MELISSA ALLRED

HANNAH

New to This Edition: A Personal Reflection on the Body and Faith

While this book is based on the story of Hannah found in the Bible, I have taken some creative liberties to bring the story to life. I have drawn on various sources, including the Midrash and Aggadah, and used my imagination to flesh out the characters and scenes. However, I have done my best to stay true to the essence of the story and to honor its message. While I used Bible verses throughout the story, they are not necessarily in canonical order. I used certain verses, including ones from the book of Revelation as well as Psalms, to enhance the story and make it more impactful, even though they may not have been known or read by the people in Hannah's time, and they are not in historical order.

It is important to me that my readers acknowledge the sources from which I have drawn, and that I clarify any changes or adaptations that I have made to the original material. I want to be sure that I have honored the essence of the story while making it engaging for modern readers. I have also tried to do my best to give credit and acknowledgment to the various authors or content creators with whom I found my historical data and cultural information. If anything was missed by accident I will make a new addition with the corrections. I didn't intentionally misrepresent anyone maliciously. —Melissa Allred 2023

Second edition

Editing by Angela Yuriko-Smith

This book was professionally typeset on Reedsy.
Find out more at reedsy.com

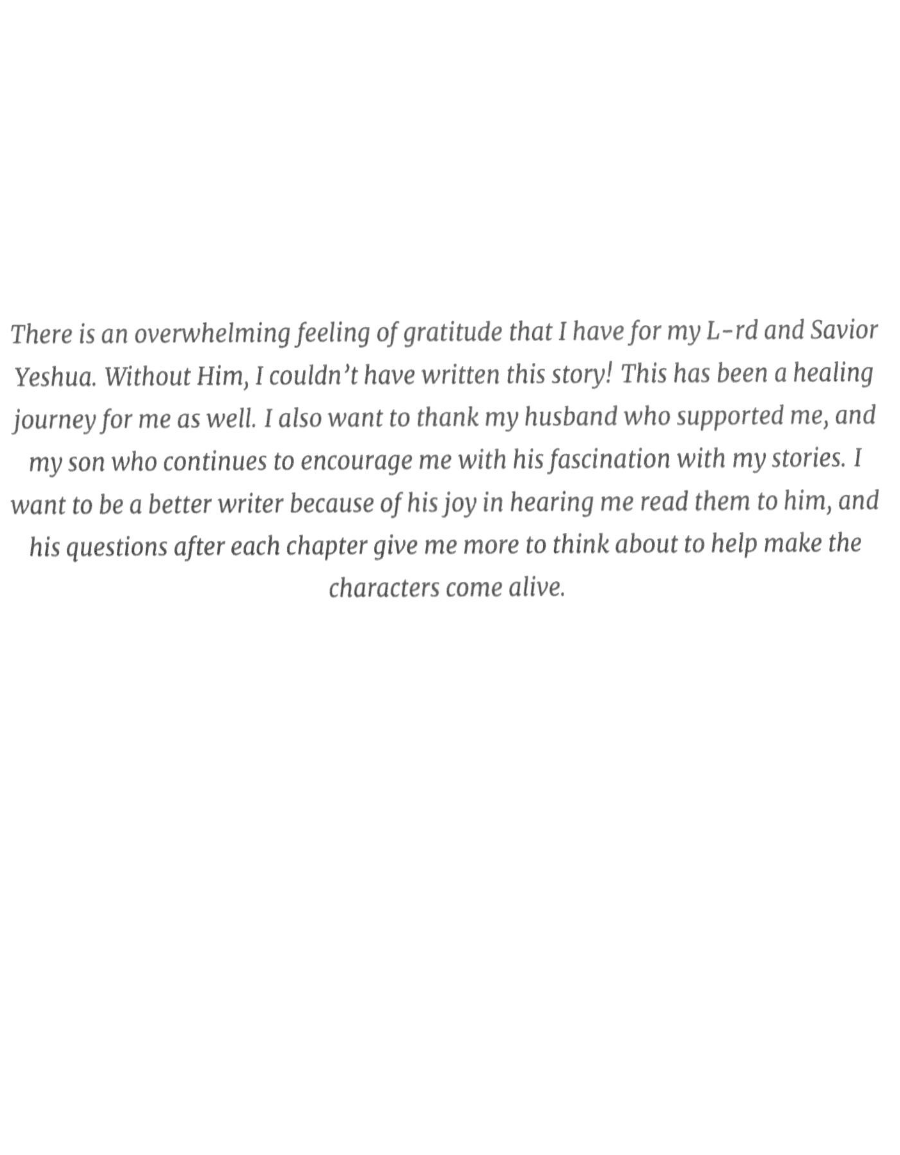

There is an overwhelming feeling of gratitude that I have for my L–rd and Savior Yeshua. Without Him, I couldn't have written this story! This has been a healing journey for me as well. I also want to thank my husband who supported me, and my son who continues to encourage me with his fascination with my stories. I want to be a better writer because of his joy in hearing me read them to him, and his questions after each chapter give me more to think about to help make the characters come alive.

"Give thanks to the L-rd, for he is good! His faithful love endures forever."

The Holy Bible

1 Chronicles 16:34 NLT

Contents

Preface

I wrote this story about Hannah for all the women in the world who are struggling with infertility, or the loss of a child. This is also my story. Hannah has always fascinated me as a biblical character. And I identified with her even as a child. Later I would struggle with infertility as well as miscarriages. And for many years my prayers seemed to go unanswered. I questioned Yahweh and sometimes lost trust in His overall goodness. I'd do things, for example, helping the homeless or less fortunate to get His attention. I'd volunteer my time and energy to get His favor. After our last miscarriage in 2014, I was in a dark place in my faith. Yet, I held on to Yahweh with all my might!

In 2016 a divine appointment at my job set me and my husband on a path to adoption. We didn't know the journey would take three more years, as we had to also go through brokenness to understand what adoption truly is. In March 2018 we met our son. I knew the instant that he was in my arms, that he was my child! And we formed a quick bond. We were able to officially make him our son in February 2019. But the road to that point was always paved with uncertainty up until the day that it was official. We had to trust that Yahweh had a plan for all three of us. Our son is the Samuel that I prayed for. He didn't have to come from my body to be the answer to my prayer. "For this Child I prayed and Yahweh Heard".

Acknowledgments

[1]I would like to acknowledge the inspiration that I drew from the songs Which helped to shape my writing process and influenced a particular element of my story: *Blessings By Laura Story, Jireh by Elevation Worship & Maverick City, El Roi by Songs of a Sojourner–Lori Basil Brown, and Common Hymnal Unproduced | Who You Say You Are | Kierre Bjorn, Jenny Wahlstrom, Isaac Gill.*

References:

Kaufman, Michael. "Before the Jewish Wedding Ceremony."

My Jewish Learning,

https://www.myjewishlearning.com/article/before-the-jewish-wedding-ceremony/.

∧ **3;** Chanda.org. "Greeting the Bride and Groom."

The Bible. New International Version. Zondervan, 2011.

∧**6;**https://en.wikipedia.org/wiki/Hashem; Adonai, Hashem, and Adoshem (markfoster.net)

Crucible Definition & Meaning - Merriam-Webster; What does crucible mean in the Bible? | - Soccer Agency

Cited Resources:

Holy Bible: New Living Translation. Tyndale House

Publishers, Inc., 2004.

Bible. Complete Jewish Bible, David H. Stern, Jewish

New Testament Publications, Inc., 1998.

The Complete Jewish Bible was translated by David H. Stern

and published in 1998 by Jewish New Testament

∧ **9,15,23;** Arthur, Kay. L-rd I Want to Know You. Devotional Study on the Names of G-D

WaterBrook Press, 2000

^**10;** Chabad.org. "Birkat Hamazon in English." Accessed 14 Apr. 2023,https://www.chabad.org/library/article_cdo/aid/135366/jewish/Birkat-Hamazon-in-English.htm

^**39-40;** "Hannah: Midrash and Aggadah." Jewish Women's Archive, https://jwa.org/encyclopedia/article/hannah-midrash-and-aggadah. Accessed 14 Apr. 2023.

^**34** 40 Days - Divinely Intended Mates (mesora.org)

2

MY BELOVED IS MINE AND I AM HIS

Hannah, the daughter of the Levite Eleazar, was in her room getting ready for her wedding. Her heart was fluttering with excitement, and she could barely contain her joy. Every time she glanced at her dress or felt the flowers in her hair, she giggled, imagining the moment she would stand under the chuppah with her beloved. Her mother, sisters, and aunts were bustling around her, each one contributing to her transformation.

As they added delicate flowers to her hair, Hannah's laughter filled the room, contagious and effervescent. The air was thick with anticipation and happiness. Her sisters teased her playfully, and she responded with bright, beaming smiles. Her mother's eyes shone with tears of joy as she adjusted the final touches on Hannah's dress. The energy was infectious, a blend of loving support and unrestrained celebration.

Hannah had been betrothed to Elkhana since she was twelve years old. He was a noble and prominent member of the Levitical order. A prophet, he feared G-D. Elkhana lived in the mountains of Ephraim. He was the son of Jeroham, who was the son of Elihu, who was the son of Tohu, who was the son of Zips.

His faithfulness to G-D and his duty to his family made him a respected man at the gates. Today Hannah would marry this man, she barely knew, but had prepared her whole life for. She was a righteous young woman and very beautiful. Her marriage to Elkhana would bring her family to a higher position in the Levitical community, where her father, Eleazar, served in the temple as a musician. Her father would now be allowed to sit with other respected men in the synagogue as well as read the Torah during the Sabbath. This was a great honor. Hannah's mother, Rachel, would also be highly esteemed among the other women. This was an advantageous union!

The excitement extended outside to where all the men gathered to congratulate the happy groom. Elkhana was still trying to figure out how he had been so blessed to have been matched to such a bright and beautiful young woman as Hannah. Today he would take her as his wife. The future was as bright as the noonday sun shining above him now. Men danced around him in a circle in a raptured frenzy.

"Today is the day the L-rd has made," Elkhana kept saying. He was rejoiced in this day that G-D had given him. His heart was so full it was about to burst! He got up to make a speech.

"My brethren, thank you for supporting me today on this glorious occasion. I want to tell you how very happy I am to be leaving the ranks of a bachelor." Many laughed.

"O, how the mighty have fallen!" One of his friends jeered.

Elkhana laughed too. "I've fallen for sure, Elijah, for the fairest of maidens in the land has captured my heart and I've been helpless to resist her!" They all toasted him with raised cups, smiles and slaps on each other's backs.

"Someone stop him from making a fool of himself!" One of his friends jumped up as a few other friends also joined in and they rushed for Elkhana and picked him up and began to parade him around the circle as they all began to whoop and holler once again.

"Don't speak anymore, you love sick bird!" Another friend chided playfully. "Or else your bride will think that she's married a simpleton." Everyone was enjoying the roasting, even Elkhana. It was all in jest, a way to lighten the nerves of the groom, and it worked.

Inside the house, the women had moved to the sitting area. Hannah was now waiting to be blessed by her father and other prominent men in her family. She was sitting on several large cushions as her wedding guests gathered around her to give her gifts and advice.

Hannah was filled with nervous energy. She was sad to leave her parents and the only home she'd ever known, but she was ready to be Elkhana's wife, and move to his home in Ephraim.

As she thought about her new life to come she said a quick prayer, "Blessed art thou, O L-rd, King of the universe my heart is filled with wonderful joy, I am in awe of your goodness to me. For who am I to be given such a blessing as a good and righteous husband as Elkhana? But, my heart is also afraid. You are not the author of fear, for such love has no fear, because perfect love expels all fear. If we are afraid, it is for fear of punishment, and this shows that we have not fully experienced your perfect love. [1] This is my wedding day! Grant to me that the joy of this day and the wonder and the beauty will never grow dark or cold. I pray that the memories will always remind us all the more of this sweet and tender occasion, and that with each passing anniversary we will be steadfastly more in love than the previous years."

It was now time to sign the ketubah. The Rabbi approached Hannah, and together with her parents, they made their way to where Elkhana was waiting. Hannah's face was veiled, but Elkhana could feel her emotions, as they matched his own. Eleazar lifted his daughter's veil so that Elkhana and the witnesses could see that she wasn't an impostor. This was a tradition that began after Jacob was deceived by his father-in-law Laban and he was secretly married to Leah instead of her sister Rachel, whom Jacob had worked seven years for. Jacob didn't know that he had been tricked until the wedding night and he had to work seven more years to obtain Rachel's hand.

Elkhana smiled when he saw his bride's face. He quoted a verse to her and the witnesses. "You are beautiful, my darling, beautiful beyond words. Your eyes are like doves behind your veil. Your hair falls in waves, like a flock of goats winding down the slopes of Gilead. Your teeth are as white as sheep, recently shorn and freshly washed. Your smile is flawless, each tooth matched with its twin. Your lips are like a scarlet ribbon; your mouth is inviting. Your cheeks are like rosy pomegranates behind your veil. Your neck is as beautiful as the tower of Zion, jeweled with the shields of a thousand heroes." [2]

As he said these words, he lightly touched her hand and they sat down together. While the cantor began to read their contract, Hannah shyly returned his gesture and squeezed his hand. After they signed their contract, Elkhana placed the veil back over Hannah's face. He made his way with his parents to stand under the Chuppah. Hannah was escorted by her parents to stand next to Elkhana. With her mother she circled Elkhana seven times to symbolize a wall of love, which was an everlasting spiritual and emotional protection around the couple.

Hands raised, the rabbi called a blessing to her and Elkhana. "Blessed and welcome! He who is mightier than all; He who is blessed above all; He who is greater than all; He who is distinguished beyond all; He should bless the groom and the bride." [3]

The ceremony seemed to go by in a blur. They received their seven blessings and drank wine from the shared cup. As Elkhana placed the ring on Hannah's hand, she realized that nothing would ever be the same again. She was and forever would be Elkhana's wife.

She whispered a silent prayer as the Rabbi blessed them once again. "I am my beloved's and my beloved is mine."

The rabbi gave the invitation to the wedding feasts shouting, "Yet in the towns of Judah and the streets of Shiloh that are deserted, inhabited by neither people nor animals, there will be heard once more the sounds of joy and gladness, the voices of bride and bridegroom." [4] He gestured to the place where the tables were set up with a magnificent feast. "Come let us celebrate with the happy couple!"

The guests all joined in and said "For the wedding of the Lamb has come, and His bride has made herself ready. Blessed are those who are invited to the wedding supper of the Lamb!" [5]

The celebration lasted for several days and then it was time for Hannah and Elkhana to go to Ephraim. Hannah held onto her mother Rachel, crying. She was broken hearted to leave her, but at the same time, there was hope in her heart. Rachel held her daughter close, feeling the pain of separation but also a sense of joy and pride for Hannah's new life with her husband.

As they said their goodbyes, Rachel whispered words of encouragement and love to her daughter, reminding her of G-D's faithfulness and provision. "May your union always bring glory to Hashem, [6] and may you rejoice in one another. HaShem bless you and keep you and make His face shine upon you and your family for a thousand generations to come. May laughter fill your hearts and may your home soon be filled with the sounds of happy children. Now go forth loving HaShem, and each other all the days of your lives. Seeking

Him first thing each new day together, in all your ways acknowledge Him, and he will make a straight path for you.[7] When you face challenges do not seek to face them alone; but do so, hand in hand, knowing that with Hashem, together you will through His grace, conquer any obstacle that may arise together."

Rachel hugged Hannah for the last time and then released her daughter to her new life. Despite her sadness, Hannah felt a glimmer of hope in her heart as she and Elkhana began their journey to Ephraim. She knew that G-D had a plan for her life, and she trusted that He would guide and protect her every step of the way.

SETTING UP HOUSEKEEPING

Hannah had been married for several weeks, and as she began to settle into her new life with Elkhana, she found herself feeling overwhelmed by the responsibilities of being a wife and homemaker. Growing up in her father's house, she helped her mother, along with her sisters, who had shared the burden of care for most of the household tasks. Now, she was faced with the challenge of setting up her own home and taking care of her husband's needs all on her own.

Hannah's days were filled with various household chores and tending to their small garden, as well as caring for their few chickens and goats. Milking alone consumed a significant portion of her time, as their two goats and their young had to be regularly moved to different areas of their property for grazing, and milked twice a day. She also had to make sure that they had clean clothes to wear. Hannah often felt exhausted by the time dinner rolled around each evening. Nonetheless, Elkhana was always patient with her and encouraged her efforts.

Despite her efforts, Hannah still felt insecure and doubtful, especially when she couldn't complete everything on time. No matter what difficulties she faced, Hannah remained committed to fashioning a loving and hospitable environment within their home. She poured her heart and soul into each task, whether it was cooking a meal, tending to the garden, or mending clothes. As time passed, she gained confidence in her abilities and took pride in the home she had created with Elkhana.

One afternoon, Hannah was cleaning her home. She began to recite a verse while she admired the structure of the house that Elkhana had built for her. He had taken a few extra years after their betrothal to complete it. And while he was building it, she waited for him at her parent's home, anticipating the day he would make the announcement that it was ready, and then they would be married.

Their house was very sturdy and the foundation was sound. She was running her hands over the details in the wall as she said: "Fragrant cedar branches are the beams of our house, and pleasant smelling firs are the rafters."[8] She murmured, savoring the words. The verse spoke to her of the beauty and strength of their home, as well as the love that had gone into its construction. As she worked, Hannah felt a sense of peace and contentment settling over her. She placed her hand on her belly and prayed a prayer for her yet-to-be children.

"O L-rd, King of the universe, will you please grant me the gift of a son? I pray that I will be able to raise him up for you and that he will be respected at the gates just as his father is. May he grow up to serve you all the days of his life." She felt a surge of emotion. Hannah longed for a child, a precious gift from G-D that would fill their home with love and joy. Her prayer was heartfelt and sincere, and she poured all of her hopes and dreams into it. She knew that having a child was not in her own power but in G-D's hands. And so, she trusted in Him to fulfill her deepest longing and to bless her and her husband with the precious gift of a child.

Elkhana came home shortly after and was looking for his meal. Hannah busied herself with getting his plate prepared and then she took her own plate and filled it up with her warm lentil stew and fresh home-baked bread. She was forever grateful that her mother had taught her the fine art of baking bread. The stew was hot and delicious. Elkhana slurped it hungrily, and she smiled at his enjoyment of it.

"My love that was an amazing meal! You have added to my life with your goodness and great skills in the kitchen." Elkhana complimented her. Hannah blushed. He lifted his hand up and said the after-meal prayer of thanks: "Blessed are You, L-rd, King of the universe, who, in His goodness, provides sustenance for the entire world with grace, with kindness, and with mercy.

He gives food to all flesh, for His kindness is everlasting. Through His great goodness to us continuously we do not lack food, and may we never lack food, for the sake of His great Name. For He, benevolent Elohim,[9] provides nourishment and sustenance for all, does good to all, and prepares food for all His creatures whom He has created, as it is said: You open Your hand and satisfy the desire of every living thing. Blessed are You, L-rd, Who provides food for all."[10]

"How was your day, my dear?" Elkhana inquired.

She smiled and replied, "It was a busy day, but I managed to get everything done. I cleaned the house, washed the clothes, and prepared dinner for us."

Elkhana nodded approvingly. "You are a hard worker, my dear. I am blessed to have you as my wife."

Hannah bowed her head in acknowledgment and replied, "I am blessed to have you as my husband, Elkhana. You have provided for me a beautiful home and have been kind to me."

Elkhana took her hand and said, "I will always provide for you and protect you, my love. And together, we will build a life that honors G-D and bring joy to our hearts." Hannah smiled, grateful for the love and support of her husband, and the hope of a future filled with the blessings of G-D. He finished and then continued: "My mother would like to come to visit tomorrow if this is okay with you?"

He questioned cautiously. He wanted her to know that this was her home and that she had a say in how she managed it. As Hannah was clearing the supper plates away she looked at her sweet husband with respect, "Yes I would love to have her over, I miss being able to talk to people." And with that, Elkhana hugged his wife around the waist.

He kissed the nape of her neck and said, "You don't have to always be alone here keeping house my love. Go to the village and meet with the other women, and make some new friends! This is now your community." She turned and smiled up at him. He was so tall and very handsome!

"I believe I'll do that after your mother visits tomorrow." She replied. Elkhana smiled at her response, happy to see her taking the initiative in building relationships with the community.

"That's a wonderful idea, my dear," he said, kissing her forehead. "I want you to be happy and have meaningful relationships here." Hannah smiled and leaned into him, feeling grateful for his love and support.

"Thank you, Elkhana. You are always so kind to me." They finished cleaning up the kitchen together, chatting about their plans for the upcoming week, and sharing stories about their childhood. As they went to bed that night, Hannah felt content and grateful for the life she was building with her husband, and the hope of a future filled with love, family, and faith.

The next afternoon Judith knocked on Hannah's door. She had a basket of fresh vegetables from her garden to share with the newlyweds. Hannah had only just started on her garden and so it would be several more weeks before she could harvest anything from it for their table. She thanked Judith and then went to work making a quick snack of walnuts and apples for them to enjoy while they visited. She also poured Judith a cup of wine that was sent with them from their wedding, a sweet reminder of that beautiful day.

"Your house is coming along beautifully daughter," Judith beamed with pride. Her son had built a strong and handsome home. She was biased of course. Hannah smiled warmly, feeling grateful for the compliment from her mother-in-law.

"Thank you, Judith. We are very happy here."

Judith took a sip of wine and then said "Please, call me mother, Hannah...It would make me very happy." She looked at Hannah with a serious expression.

Hannah dipped her head with shy respect and in agreement replied "Okay, thank you, Mother." It sounded foreign to her ears, but it was nice.

"How are you adjusting to married life?" Judith inquired. Hannah took a deep breath, knowing that Judith was genuine in asking about her well-being.

"It's been an adjustment, to be sure. But I'm learning every day, and Elkhana is such a patient and kind teacher." Judith nodded in understanding.

"Marriage is a partnership, my daughter. You and Elkhana are a team, and you must work together to build a happy and fulfilling life together." Hannah took a sip of her wine and thought about Judith's words. She knew that building a life with Elkhana would take time and effort, but she was ready for the challenge. And with her faith in G-D and the support of her new family, she knew she could overcome any obstacle. They visited for a few hours, and then Judith left. Hannah sighed as she watched her leave. She missed her own mother who lived several days away, but maybe she could learn to appreciate Judith, and maybe possibly even love her half as much as she loved her own mother. As Hannah cleaned up the kitchen, Elkhana entered the room.

"How was your visit with my mother?" He asked. Hannah turned to face him, a soft smile on her lips.

"It was lovely. She brought over some fresh vegetables from her garden and we had a nice chat."

Elkhana nodded, pleased. "I'm glad to hear it. She's a wonderful woman, my mother."

Hannah smiled in agreement. "Yes, she is. I think I'm going to try to make more of an effort to get to know her better."

Elkhana's face lit up at her words. "That's wonderful to hear, my love. I'm sure she'll be thrilled." Hannah smiled and took his hand, squeezing it gently.

"Thank you for being such a kind and patient husband." Elkhana leaned in to give her a quick kiss. "I love you, Hannah."

"I love you too," she replied, feeling grateful for everything she had been blessed with. Then she turned and began to make dinner. She couldn't wait to savor the fresh vegetables that her mother-in-law showered them with.

THE FIRST OF MANY SORROWS

Hannah kept her promise to Elkhana to meet with the other women in the village. She soon made friends with Leah who was close to her age and was also newly married. They found that they had a lot in common and became fast friends. She invited Leah over to her house where they would sew and knit, and while they worked, they would share their hopes and dreams for the future.

They talked about their desire to have children and raise them to honor G-D. They shared stories about their families and childhoods and laughed over shared experiences. Hannah was grateful for the friendship that was growing between them and felt less lonely in her new home.

Leah also introduced Hannah to some of the other women in the village, and soon she was invited to join a group of women who gathered together to pick wild fruits and berries in the surrounding area. As they picked berries, the women would often sing songs of worship and praise to G-D, and Hannah found comfort in their words. They would sit together in the tall grass and have little picnics as they shared stories and advice.

She was grateful for the community of women who accepted her and lifted her up, reminding her that she was loved and valued. Through this experience, Hannah learned the importance of fellowship and the power of G-Dly friendships. She found herself looking forward to the weekly companionship.

Through her daily routines and the camaraderie with the other women, Hannah began to find a sense of purpose and fulfillment. She began to see how her work and her presence in the community were valuable and important. As the weeks went by, Hannah began to feel more comfortable in her new home and community. She continued to spend time with Leah and the other women, and they began to rely on each other for support and encouragement. They prayed for each other and shared their struggles and victories. Hannah was grateful for the sense of belonging she felt among them.

One cold rainy day, while Hannah was making bread, a courier arrived. The letter said that she was needed back home as soon as possible. Her father had become very sick. The message said to make all haste. She showed it to Elkhana when he returned home from the city gates that evening. His face showed deep concern as he read the message.

"Of course, my love. We will make arrangements to leave first thing in the morning. I will send word to my mother asking her to stay here and watch over the house for us while we are away." Hannah nodded, feeling a mix of anxiety and sadness. She was worried about her father and the journey ahead, and saddened to leave behind her home and her new friends.

The next morning, they gathered their belongings and made their way back to Hannah's childhood home. The journey was long and arduous, but they finally arrived after several days of travel. Hannah's mother welcomed them warmly, but it was clear that her father's condition was grave. Hannah spent every moment at his bedside, praying and caring for him. But despite her best efforts, he passed away after only a few days.

The weeks that followed were a blur of grief and mourning. Hannah felt adrift without her father, but Elkhana was a constant source of comfort and support. He took care of all the arrangements and made sure that Hannah's mother Rachel and youngest sister Dinah were taken care of.

Rachel was surrounded by the love and support of her family. She was grateful to be taken in by Joshua her son-in-law, and to be able to live with her daughter Ruth and their children, but her grief was still so debilitating that she spent many days in bed. It was hard for Hannah to leave her and go back to Ephraim with Elkhana, but Rachel assured her that her place was there, and she needed to make her life with Elkhana. Finally, it was time to return to their own home in Ephraim. It was a bittersweet moment for Hannah, as she was leaving behind the place where she had grown up and where her father had passed away, but also returning to her new home with her beloved husband.

Despite the kindness of her family, Rachel found it difficult to adjust to her new life as a widow. She missed her husband terribly and often found herself overcome with grief. Dinah also struggled with the changes in their family dynamic. She had to take on new responsibilities, such as caring for her nieces and nephews and helping her sister Ruth with household chores. As she was the youngest in her family, she was used to getting away with things and being a free spirit, but now she had responsibilities, and with her mother sick in bed most days, it made her angry that she had to take on so much.

Hannah, who had now settled back at her home with Elkhana, worried about her mother and sister. She prayed for them often, asking G-D to comfort them and provide for their needs.

One day, Hannah received a letter from Joshua, telling her that Rachel's health had taken a turn for the worse. She had developed a persistent cough and was having trouble breathing. Hannah was deeply concerned and immediately sent a messenger to her mother with some herbs and remedies that she thought might help.

She tried to go about daily life as before, but her heart was heavy with grief and worry as well. Why would Elohim choose to take her father from her, she questioned. She spent time in prayer as she washed the clothes and hung them to dry.

"My heart, O Adonai is steadfast, my heart is steadfast; I will sing and make music, I will thank you, L-rd, among all the people. I will sing your praises among the nations. For your unfailing love is as high as the heavens. Your faithfulness reaches to the skies be exalted, O G-D, above the highest heavens. May your glory shine over all the earth.[11]

I want to understand why there is so much sadness and pain in this world! But I won't be unfaithful to you, O L-rd my rock. Please help me to accept this as your will. I loved, and still love my father. Now his soul rests in your presence. I will praise you and offer my thanksgiving, for the time that you gave me with my earthly father. Please do not take offense that I mourn for him. And please do not hold it against me that I don't understand your ways.

My soul is weary from crying and I desire to be comforted, please heal my mother and help her in her sadness as well." Hannah felt a little better as weeks went by. She was still sad, but not consumed by it. Her prayers were healing. And G-D was faithful to comfort her.

A few months had passed since Eleazar's death; Leah was helping Hannah at her house to prepare a meal to share with a friend who had just given birth. They talked excitedly about the new baby, as well as their desire to soon have little ones. They looked at one another, puzzled, by an unexpected knock at the door.

When Hannah opened the door to greet her visitor; her heart sank, as he handed her another message from her hometown. She could not bear to open the letter. Leah was right beside her and had to steady Hannah so she didn't fall over. Leah thanked the man, paid him, then closed the door. She escorted Hannah to a chair and then poured her a glass of water.

Hannah asked her friend to read it, and if it bore bad news, to wait until Elkhana came home before she shared it with them. Hannah had a bad feeling. She didn't have to wait long to find out what was in the letter; as Elkhana came home early that day. Leah handed him the message this time and told him that Hannah hadn't read the letter and didn't know its contents.

Elkhana's face fell as he read the letter and looked at Hannah. He thanked Leah for her kindness and then asked if he could be alone with his wife. She gave Hannah a reassuring hug and whispered "I'm here when you need me." She picked up her basket and left their home. As she walked down the path she heard Hannah wailing, and her heart broke in two for her dear friend. Hannah's mother had also died from a broken heart. She was now an orphan.

They made the familiar journey back to her childhood home once again. Her sisters along with their husbands and their children, all gathered to say goodbye. And then, all too soon, Hannah and Elkhana returned to their own home in Ephraim.

Darkness was setting in over Hannah's perfect happy ending. She began to lose sleep, and couldn't eat. And soon she was not able to keep up with her daily housekeeping as before. Losing her father tested her faith and resolve. But losing her mother shortly after him was too much for her heart to endure.

Being so far from home made it worse, as she felt that she couldn't grieve properly. Judith would visit her regularly and help her around the house and in the garden. She would recite verses of comfort to Hannah. Leah, along with the other women in the village, provided warm meals for Hannah and Elkhana. Their generosity touched Hannah deeply. She knew that she could find healing through the support of her family and her friends.

Leah, true to her word, didn't leave Hannah alone to grieve. They cried and prayed together. She was a genuine friend. "I don't understand what Elohim expects from me, Leah", Hannah said one day while they mended some of Elkhana's garments. "When my father passed away, I was very hurt. But I wasn't especially angry at Him. I did have questions I felt needed to be answered. But in the end, Elohim gave me his comfort. Now...," she paused, and thought for a minute, "Now, I am just angry!"

Leah placed her hand lovingly on top of Hannah's and nodded in empathy. She prayed quietly to herself for her friend. But she didn't offer council. She just listened to Hannah as she shared her pain. And for Hannah, this was enough. Her anger kept bumping into her faith and she had to wonder if Elohim was still good. At that moment He didn't seem good, and she was upset at herself for her doubts and fears.

It caused her to be emotionally torn and distant towards Elkhana too, because he was a very faithful and devout Jew and was a prominent leader in their community. He served at the gates as an advisor and elder. He was respected and highly favored. At night he would read the Torah to her and pray over her. But she would be inwardly screaming at him to stop, because the words were not washing over her, and she wasn't experiencing the peace that he said would be available through Hashem's words.

Elkhana was reading the book of Job one night and just mentioned in passing that "The L-rd restored Job's fortunes when he prayed on behalf of his friends, and the L-rd gave Job twice what he had before." This upset Hannah who knew the story well enough. Yes the L-rd did give Job back what he lost. And he did give Job more children. But was G-D going to give Hannah another father or mother? She was very tired of hearing about what He was able to do. She just wanted her mother!

Was He going to raise her back from the dead? She fumed to herself. Elkhana looked up from his reading, noticing the pain etched on Hannah's face. He knew her grief was still raw, but he also knew that she needed to process it and find a way to move forward.

"Hannah," he said gently, "I know it hurts. But we have to trust that Hashem has a plan for us, even in the midst of our pain. He may not bring back what we've lost, but He can bring healing and comfort if we let Him." He paused, then added, "Let's pray together and ask Him to give us the strength to trust, and to find peace in His love."

Hannah softened somewhat as Elkhana took her hand. She was grateful for a G-Dly husband. She did try not to let it cast a dark cloud over her marriage and relationship, but her soul was aching deep within and she didn't know how to pray or how to tell her husband that she was angry at G-D. Her sorrow was still so deep, Hannah hated that she felt like this, but it would take more than just words from Job to cleanse her wounds.

Judith, her mother-in-law always had the right verses for her. Judith would help Hannah with her chores and hum a tune that sounded familiar to Hannah. One day she asked her what it was. Judith sang a little verse: "Heal me, L-rd, and I will be healed; save me and I will be saved, for you are the one I praise. Create in me a pure heart, O G-D, and renew a steadfast spirit within my flesh. My heart may fail, but G-D is the strength of my heart and my portion forever." ^12,13,14

As the days passed, Hannah continued to struggle with her grief and anger toward G-D. She found comfort in the presence of her friend Leah and the wise words of her mother-in-law Judith. But she still couldn't shake off the feeling of emptiness and loss that consumed her every day. One day, while walking along the riverbank, Hannah saw a woman sitting by the water, weeping uncontrollably. She felt drawn to her and approached her gently. The woman looked up, surprised, and Hannah could see the pain etched on her face. Without saying a word, Hannah sat down next to her and took her hand. They sat there in silence for a while, the woman's tears slowly subsiding as they both watched the river flow.

After some time, the woman spoke. "My husband passed away a few months ago," she said, her voice barely above a whisper. "We were married for over thirty years, and I feel lost without him. I don't know how to go on."

Hannah listened attentively, feeling a sense of kinship with this stranger who was going through the same pain she was. As they talked, Hannah shared her own struggles with grief and anger toward G-D. The woman nodded in understanding, and they both cried together.

It was a powerful moment of connection, and Hannah realized that maybe her pain had a purpose after all. Maybe she was meant to help others who were going through the same thing. In the weeks that followed, Hannah continued to meet with the woman by the river, and they became good friends.

They would talk about their husbands, their families, and their faith. Hannah found that helping others with their pain helped ease her own. She started to see a glimmer of hope in the midst of her sorrow.

A GLIMMER OF HOPE

One afternoon, Leah knocked at Hannah's door, her face was glowing. She had glorious news to share with her best friend. She was pregnant! Hannah smiled and gave Leah a hug.

"The L-rd is so good! He's heard our prayers," said Leah ecstatically.

Hannah replied. "The L-rd bless you and keep you through this time." But inside she felt a sting of jealousy because she had expected to have news by now of her own pregnancy. So far, it was not to be.

Leah noticed the change in Hannah's demeanor and asked, "Is everything alright?"

Hannah forced a smile. "Of course, I am happy for you, Leah. It's just that...," she trailed off, not wanting to burden her friend with her struggles.

But Leah persisted, "Just what, Hannah? You can tell me anything."

Hannah took a deep breath. "It's just that, Elkhana and I have been trying for a baby too, but it hasn't happened yet." Leah's face softened and she took Hannah's hand,

"I'm so sorry, But you must remember that the L-rd has a plan for each of us, and in His own time, He will grant you the gift of a child as well."

Hannah nodded, trying to accept her friend's words. She knew that Leah was right and that she needed to have faith in G-D's plan for her life. But her anger at him was causing a chasm that she didn't know could be repaired. She sighed.

"Thank you. You always know just what to say. And I am very happy for you!" She gave Leah another hug. Leah promised to pray for Hannah and

Elkhana to have a child. As Leah left, Hannah watched her go, feeling a sense of sadness, she knew that she needed to repair her faith and trust in the L-rd, and that in so doing, He would guide her through whatever trials lay ahead.

"Adonai, [15] please forgive me for doubting you, and even for my anger towards you. For your ways are not our ways, Your Thoughts are not our thought.[16] When I consider your heavens, the work of your fingers, the moon, and the stars which you have set in place, what is mankind that you are mindful of them, human beings that you care for them?"[17]

She knelt down in her garden and began to pull weeds as she continued to pour her heart out in prayer. "You have made them a little lower than the angels and crowned them with glory and honor. You made them rulers over the works of your hands you put everything under their feet: all flocks and herds, and the animals of the wild, the birds in the sky, and the fish in the sea, all that swim the paths of the seas. L-rd, our L-rd, how majestic is your name in all the earth! [18]

As Hannah worked and prayed, her soul felt as if it was being washed by heavenly rain. She looked up into the sky searching for a cloud, thinking about how the rain would wash over her garden and restore it. That was like praise, and giving worship to Elohim, she thought to herself. It caused her heart and soul to feel refreshed and new. The garden of her soul was able to grow deeper roots. This was a brand new revelation for her.

She began to cry again, her tears splashing on the dry dirt below her. "Be merciful to me, L-rd, for I am in distress; my eyes grow weak with sorrow, my soul and body with grief. Though You bring grief, You will show compassion, so great is Your unfailing love. For You do not willingly bring affliction or grief to anyone. Yet this I call to mind and therefore I have hope: Because of the L-rd's great love, we are not consumed, for his compassion never fails. They are new every morning; great is your faithfulness. [19-21]

Several weeks had passed, and Leah was now showing. It was a constant reminder to Hannah of something she didn't have. And Elkhana noticed that she wasn't as cheerful as she once had been. He knew the burden she carried with the loss of her parents and he did his best to comfort her, but as a man, he just didn't understand the immense burden that Hannah felt as a childless woman. He was still very kind, but his level of support in this situation was lacking. Hannah was grateful for Elkhana's kindness, but she still felt alone in her struggle with infertility. She began to pour her heart out to the L-rd, crying out to Him for a child. She went to the synagogue daily and prayed fervently, tears streaming down her face.

One afternoon Judith saw her there and took her hand, thinking she was grieving over her parents. While she was, Hannah was also grieving over her inadequacies as a woman. She felt like a failure. Judith held her hand while she cried. She knew that Hannah had to work the grief out in her way. Hannah wiped away her tears and looked at Judith.

"Thank you for being here with me, Mother," Hannah said, her voice still quavering with emotion.

Judith nodded sympathetically. "I can't imagine how hard it must be for you, Hannah. Losing both your parents at such a young age..." Her voice trailed off as she squeezed Hannah's hand tighter.

"I do miss my parents, but I know that they are resting in heaven. I do need my mother so much right now!" She said, choking back tears. "I've trusted Hashem since I was a child. And everyone keeps telling me that He has a plan for me. Even if I don't understand it right now. But this is such a hard journey that I'm on. It's lonely." She began to sob again.

Judith nodded and gave her a mother's hug. "You're a strong woman, Hannah," she said. "And you have a good heart. Hashem's ways are beyond finding out. It isn't that we just say "I trust you L-rd..." she paused thinking how to best comfort Hannah. "It's not enough to say you know He has a plan for you. You have to know Him, daughter, you have to see His goodness, as well as the trials He gives you as gifts. He is in the refining and in the waiting too." She explained. "When you know He is good, even in the hard times, you know that it will all work out for the best of those who love Him, and are called by Him. Hashem looks for a soul as beautiful as yours and decides that he wants to make it into a priceless precious treasure. You will not see it while you are in the furnace, but eventually, you'll be able to say that you can see His goodness in the land of the living. And you'll know Him better. You'll be able to help another woman who will be blessed by your story." Judith spoke with encouragement.

Hannah shared with Judith about her friend Mary, whom she had met earlier by the river, and how the two were able to console one another in their grief. Judith listened intently to Hannah's words, nodding in understanding.

"It sounds like Mary is a true friend to you, Hannah. You are blessed to have her in your life." She said with a smile.

"Yes," Hannah agreed. "She has been a source of comfort to me too. We have been able to share our struggles with one another and offer each other support." Hannah said a hint of gratitude in her voice.

"That's wonderful to hear, my dear," replied Judith, "Having someone to lean on during difficult times is so important." Judith gave her a wise smile. "But don't forget, Hannah, ultimately it is Hashem who will provide you with the strength and comfort that you need. Keep turning to Him in prayer and trust in His plan for your life. He will never leave you nor forsake you." She gave Hannah a reassuring pat on Hannah's hand. Hannah nodded, feeling a sense of peace wash over her. She felt hope return to her heart and knew that Judith was right. G-D would bless her when the time was right. She just had to trust in Him and His plan.

"Thank you Mother." She hugged Judith and looked down, unsure if she wanted to share her deepest hurt with Judith, but she knew that her mother-in-law loved her. Hannah decided to trust her.

"I've been struggling with the fact that Elkhana and I still have not conceived a child, and that is really why I am here today and crying. I see Leah, and she's close to her delivery date, in a few months! We are also coming up to our first anniversary soon and we still don't have any news. It's been hard not having my mother here to help me through this trial."

Judith, understanding now the full scope of Hannah's burden, took her by the hand again, as they left the synagogue. "Let's take a walk, daughter," she suggested. And so the women began to walk through the village. It was a nice afternoon with a breeze to ward off the heat. The market smelled of herbs and fresh bread. Hannah was hungry, so they picked something to share and sat down to enjoy their meal. After they had finished, and were satisfied, Judith turned to Hannah and told her about her own struggles to get pregnant and stay pregnant.

"Before Elkhana was born, I had already had several miscarriages." she explained. "My own sister had her babies, as well as other family members and friends. But for me, it took longer and was a struggle. And I too doubted the goodness of Hashem. I didn't understand why He gave me a woman's heart and desire to have children and not let me fulfill His command to be fruitful and multiply. I prayed too, just like you are doing now. But Elkhana came when the time was right. His siblings soon followed and I was able to fulfill my calling as a mother."

Hannah listened respectfully to Judith, happy to have someone to confide in that understood her plight. "But, Mother," she said in response. "What if Elohim never gives me that opportunity?"

She was on the verge of tears again. Judith declared that He would, "I am confident that you will see the goodness of the L-rd in the land of the living, ^22 in His own time, Hannah." She ended.

Leah was glowing. Hannah was genuinely glad for her friend. She had tirelessly sewn baby clothes for her and was delivering them to her house. Leah was overcome by the small baby items. As Hannah handed her the baby clothes, her heart was filled with joy for her friend. She couldn't wait to see Leah's little one and hold them in her arms. At the same time, Hannah's heart still ached for a child of her own, but seeing the happiness and excitement in Leah's eyes, she pushed aside her own feelings and focused on being a good friend and supporting Leah during this special time.

Leah thanked Hannah with tears in her eyes, grateful for such a thoughtful and kind friend. She couldn't wait for her baby to wear the clothes Hannah had made with so much love and care. They chatted about the upcoming arrival of Leah's baby and went over baby names. Hannah was content to be there for her friend and support her in any way she could.

Leah's delivery day arrived six weeks later, and Hannah was a mixture of emotions. She wrestled with the guilt of feeling jealous and the excitement of having a new life to guide. Leah was a natural-born mother, and her baby girl, whom she named Hadassah, resembled her in almost every way. There was so much excitement on this brand-new day, she went home feeling exhausted.

Elkhana came home and she did her best not to diminish him or his day with her grumpiness. For the most part, Elkhana didn't notice that anything was wrong with her, but he commented that she looked tired. Hannah forced a smile and replied that she was just feeling a little overwhelmed with everything that had been going on. Elkhana gave her a quick hug and told her that he was proud of her for being such a good friend to Leah. That made Hannah feel a little better.

As the days went by, Hannah visited Leah often to help with the baby and to bring her meals. She loved holding the little bundle of joy in her arms and watching Leah care for her daughter with such tenderness but she couldn't help but feel a sense of emptiness and longing in her own heart. One day, while sitting in her garden and watching the flowers sway in the breeze, Hannah decided to pour out her heart to G–D once more. She prayed with all her might, tears streaming down her face.

"I want to know you Jireh,^23 I want to see your goodness. You are enough, help me to believe that." She paused and looked at the flowers in her garden and touched a petal as she said, "You dress these lilies with beauty, and they do not labor or spin. I want to know you and trust you like these flowers, but what do you want from me? I am your handmaiden, and I live and move only as you give me the ability. But what is it that you require from me?" She pleaded. "I only have myself to give." She opened her eyes and saw Elkhana walking up the path. It was time to set the table, he would be hungry.

Hannah and Elkhana celebrated their first anniversary together along with his parents and siblings. Everyone was happy and full of congratulations for the couple. But Hannah couldn't shake the feeling that someone was missing from their party. Not just her own family; her mother, and father would have been overjoyed at this special occasion, but her mind and her body missed someone she'd never met. She just felt lonely. Her life thus far wasn't turning out how she saw it a year ago on their wedding day. Elkhana noticed her sadness and asked her what was wrong.

Hannah tried to brush it off and put on a brave face, but Elkhana knew her too well. Eventually, she opened up to him about her feelings of loneliness and the disappointment of not having children yet. Elkhana listened attentively and held her close, telling her that he loved her and that they would face whatever challenges came their way together. He reminded her of the good things they had in their lives, including their love for each other and the home they had built together.

Hannah felt comforted by his words and embraced him tightly, grateful for his unwavering support. She knew that she should be happy and not let this one desire overshadow her whole existence and so she vowed to make each new day not about what she wanted, but about how she could best serve others.

She decided that she would volunteer with her sisters-in-law to help the widows in the village. Some of the women were old and feeble, and couldn't get around very well, so twice a week she and her husband's sisters would visit these homes and bring a meal and help to clean their houses. This brought hope and joy into her heart. Hannah missed her own sisters as well, so being with Martha and Naomi brought her some small comfort.

Hannah thought about a verse in the Torah that read "She extends a helping hand to the poor and opens her arms to the needy. Blessed are those who are generous, because they feed the poor." And she began to wonder if G-D would see her good works, and bless her and Elkhana with children. "Surely He sees me now," she thought.

She remained faithful and dependable in her care for others. And Elkhana was happy to have his cheerful wife back.

THE SECOND YEAR

Leah was hosting a birthday celebration for Hadassah. Leah's swollen belly showed that she was nearing her due date. Hannah had struggled with the idea that her friend was going to have another baby, but she had quickly given that emotion to G-D and was just as excited for this new baby as she had been for Hadassah. She was not going to let her own insecurities spoil Leah's joy.

It was a small family gathering with a few close friends invited as well. Hannah didn't have time to even think about her desires. She helped Leah prepare for the party by cleaning her house and decorating it with fresh-cut flowers. As the guests arrived, Hannah welcomed them warmly, helping them find a seat and serving them food and wine.

She watched as everyone admired Hadassah, preening over her, with her proud parents beaming. Amid the celebration, Hannah noticed that Leah looked uncomfortable. She had been having contractions all day but had insisted on going through with the celebration. Hannah quietly pulled Leah aside and suggested that they go to the midwife. Leah agreed and they left their guests. With Daniel, Leah's husband in charge, and with the help of Leah's mother accompanying them, they made their way to the midwife.

Hours later, they returned with a new baby boy they named Seth. Hannah was overjoyed for Leah and her growing family. She hugged her friend and praised G-D for the safe arrival of the new baby. At that moment, all of her worries and insecurities faded away. She was filled with a sense of gratitude and contentment, knowing that G-D had blessed her with such wonderful friends and family.

In good time, Hannah and Elkhana celebrated their second year of marriage together. His family again showered them with gifts and congratulations. Hannah was happier, but she still felt a piece of her happiness was missing. She banished the thought and just enjoyed her anniversary. As the celebration wound down, Elkhana turned to Hannah and asked her how she was feeling.

She hesitated for a moment before finally admitting, "I feel like something is still missing in my life. I love being married to you, but I can't help but feel like our family is incomplete without a child."

Elkhana took her hand and gave her a gentle squeeze. "I know it's been a difficult journey for us, but we can't give up hope. Let's continue to pray and trust that Hashem will bless us with a child when the time is right."

Hannah felt a wave of gratitude wash over her at Elkhana's words. She knew he didn't completely understand the depths of her longing for a child, but his unwavering support and love meant everything to her. She smiled at him and said, "Thank you for being my rock, Elkhana. I couldn't do this without you."

A message came by courier a few weeks later. Hannah's heart skipped a beat as she opened it, but it was good news. Her sister Dinah was going to visit her and stay for several months! Oh, Hannah missed her own family. She hadn't seen them since her mother passed away and her baby sister was still unwed so she was able to stay for quite some time. Hannah made her home ready to receive her guest. This was going to be such a happy reunion!

Dinah arrived three weeks later and the two sisters embraced and held one another as tears fell from their faces. Hannah couldn't believe how grown-up Dinah was now. At sixteen she was practically a woman and she would need to be married soon but since her father passed away, her younger sister's chances of being matched to a good man also faded. Their brother-in-law, who was now Dinah's guardian, didn't have the same knack for securing a husband as her father had. Dinah also lacked the dowry to help her win a proper suitor.

Hannah was happy to have her sister with her, but she couldn't help but feel a pang of guilt at her happiness. She had a loving husband and a comfortable life, while Dinah was struggling to find a suitable match. She wished she could do more to help her sister, but she didn't know what to do.

Despite these thoughts, Hannah tried to make Dinah's stay as enjoyable as possible. They spent their days together, catching up on everything that had happened since they last saw each other. They went for walks in the countryside, baked together, and spent hours talking and laughing. It was nice having help around the house too. The chores were still never-ending.

One day, while they were sitting in the garden, Dinah confided in Hannah about her worries. She was afraid that she would never find a good husband, and that she would end up alone, destined to always rely on her sisters and their husbands for support. Hannah listened patiently and comforted her, telling her that she had faith that everything would work out. As she watched her sister, Hannah couldn't help but think about her own situation. She had been married for two years and still had no children. She felt like a failure as a wife and a woman. She didn't want to burden her sister with her problems, so she kept them to herself.

As the days turned into months, Hannah found herself becoming more and more anxious about Dinah's departure. She didn't want her sister to leave, but she knew that she couldn't keep her forever. She prayed to G-D to give her the strength to say goodbye when the time came.

Elkhana came to the rescue though. He knew of a man whose wife had died suddenly, leaving him alone with five children all under the age of ten so he had made inquiries and found that there were no other eligible women for this man to marry. A message was sent to Joshua, Dinah's guardian to see if he would bless the union, and one month later, Dinah was saying her wedding vows to Nathan, a man three times her age. Hannah couldn't help but be overjoyed as she said a prayer for her sister. She was now the mother to five children! Being the baby of the family, Dinah didn't know what she was up against.

Hannah was happy for her sister, but at the same time, she couldn't help but feel a twinge of sadness that her parents were missing such a beautiful day, but she didn't want to dampen the joy of her sister's wedding. Instead, she focused on the happy couple and their future together. The celebration lasted several days, and Hannah was happy to be able to reconnect with her own sisters as they were staying with her during the wedding celebration.

As the wedding festivities came to an end, Hannah knew that she would soon have to say goodbye to her sisters. She cherished the time they had spent together and was grateful for the memories they had made, but as they prepared to leave, Hannah felt a sense of emptiness inside her. She longed for the love and companionship of a child, and the thought of being left alone with her infertility again weighed heavily on her. But then she remembered the words that Judith spoke over her, reminding her to trust in G–D's plan and see His goodness even in the midst of difficult circumstances.

With a renewed sense of hope, Hannah continued to pray and trust that G–D had a plan for her life, even if she couldn't see it yet. And she knew that, like her sister Dinah, her own future was in G–D's hands.

Over the next few months, Hannah and Dinah spent their days together helping one another with chores and tending their gardens. They were bonding. Dinah often spoke of the challenges of raising five children and how much she missed her other sisters. Hannah was grateful that Dinah was so near now, she listened and offered words of encouragement and support. She remembered how it was being a newlywed with so much responsibility. It was daunting at times, but she encouraged Dinah to find a rhythm and have a routine for her and the children to follow.

Hannah also shared with Dinah some of the struggles she had been facing, and how she had been relying on her faith to get through them. Dinah listened intently and offered her own words of comfort and support. As they spent more time together, they became closer than ever before, and Hannah felt blessed to have such a loving and supportive sister.

The Holy week of Sukkot was approaching and Elkhana surprised his wife with the idea to make a pilgrimage to the Temple in Shiloh, where they would offer sacrifices and celebrate with other worshipers. Hannah was intrigued and asked if she could invite Dinah and her family to join them.

The two women made plans for the pilgrimage, hoping to find solace and peace in the journey. They worked together to prepare food and pack supplies for the long trip. Elkhana also made plans to have them stay over one night in Hannah's hometown to visit their family. The sisters were excited and prepared for the trip with great anticipation. They packed their bags and made sure everything was in order.

On the day of the pilgrimage, they joined a group of travelers from their village, including Peninnah and her parents Aaron and Abigail. Peninnah was a sweet eight-year-old girl, who was full of energy and she attached herself to Hannah during the long journey. She would play tag with Dinah's step-children and other games as well. Hannah enjoyed the attention from the child, Peninnah's playfulness helped to pass the time and her parents relished in their newfound freedom while they entrusted their daughter to Hannah's care.

As they walked through the hills and valleys, Hannah felt her spirits lifting. The beauty of the land and the company of her fellow pilgrims helped to ease the sorrow in her heart. She spent much of her time in prayer and meditation, seeking comfort from the divine.

The journey was not without challenges, however. They encountered steep hills and rough terrain, and at times, the heat was almost unbearable, but the group pressed on, supporting each other along the way.

When they finally arrived at the holy city of Shiloh, they ascended the hill towards the temple, Hannah couldn't help but be in awe of the grandeur that awaited them. The temple, perched high above the city, stood like a majestic megalith, its grandeur radiating with an aura of divine presence. The sight of it alone filled Hannah's heart with reverence and wonder.

As they approached the temple grounds, Hannah's eyes widened at the panoramic view that unfolded before her. The countryside stretched out beneath them, a vast expanse of rolling hills and lush fields. It was as if nature itself had prepared a magnificent amphitheater to showcase the glory of G-D's creation.

During the festival nights, as darkness fell, the hillside transformed into a breathtaking spectacle. Hundreds of campfires dotted the landscape, flickering like a million stars in the night sky. The warm glow illuminated the faces of the pilgrims, creating an atmosphere of communal celebration and devotion.

In the temple, Hannah and Elkhana immersed themselves in prayer and worship. They offered their heartfelt supplications, seeking solace and hope in the presence of the Almighty. The air was thick with reverence, as pilgrims from near and far united in their devotion, their voices rising in harmonious praise.

Beyond the temple, the small town of Shiloh beckoned Hannah and Elkhana to explore its streets and markets. The vibrant bustle of the marketplace filled their senses, as merchants displayed their wares and locals mingled in joyful camaraderie. It was a time of connection, sharing stories and experiences with fellow travelers on their spiritual journey.

In the sacred surroundings of Shiloh, Hannah found solace, inspiration, and a renewed sense of purpose. The pilgrimage had not only brought her closer to G-D, but had also deepened her bond with her husband and forged lifelong friendships with fellow pilgrims.

Hannah said a prayer on their last day, thanking G-D for the blessing He had given them, that they had been able to make the journey, for the bonds they made with their fellow travelers, and for being able to see her family. She and Elkhana remained close friends with Aaron and Abigail; Peninnah's parents.

They made the long journey back home, stopping once more for the night, and staying with Ruth, her sister, then Hannah and Elkhana returned home with hearts full of gratitude and renewed faith. The experience in Shiloh deepened their connection to G-D and strengthened their resolve to face life's challenges with unwavering trust.

Hannah was fortified by the mountaintop experience for several weeks after she and Elkhana returned home and resettled into their familiar routine. However, her joy faded when her sister Dinah visited with the news that she was expecting a child. Never once had Hannah imagined that her younger sister would have children before her!

Her countenance fell. She had been on such a high after the pilgrimage and tried hard to muster the strength to be happy for her sister, but the joy that she had after returning home quickly faded and was replaced with total and abject loathing for her own body. She put on a fake mask and pretended to be happy for her sister, but inside she wanted to scream. She felt betrayed and she was deeply angry at herself for even having these emotions.

Many nights she cried silently praying for answers. "Didn't I please you, by being obedient?" she pleaded, "Do you see me El-Roi?" She hid her face in her mattress, Elkhana sleeping next to her. "Adonai, will you remain silent? I have tried to serve you with all that I am! Where is my guilt? Let me know so that I can confess it and be healed. Let me hear of your unfailing love each morning, for I am trusting you. Show me where to walk, for I give myself to you, Teach me to do your will, for you are my L-rd. May your gracious Spirit lead me forward on a firm footing." ^24

Hannah wrestled with her failures, and she couldn't shake it off. She tried to keep busy with household tasks and volunteer work, but her mind kept drifting back to her inability to provide her husband with the one thing he wanted most.

One day, while Elkhana was away, Hannah went to the synagogue to pray. She poured out her heart to G-D, weeping and begging for a child. "Elohim, I know that You are good, and You've shown me Your greatness in Shiloh. I have to trust You. I am bringing you what I have. Will you meet me here? I am trying to believe that you are who you say You are! Why can't I just be at peace with this path that I am on? I hate the anger and bitterness growing in me over Dinah's pregnancy! Please forgive me. Teach me to do your will, for you are my L-rd. Gracious Spirit, lead me and guide me." Hannah repeated her previous prayer; feeling a little more at ease.

Elkhana arrived home and noticed that she was not her usual self though. He tried to ask her what was wrong, "Is there something I can do to help you, my love?" he asked her kindly.

"No, not really," She replied. "I am just wrestling with Hashem for the desires of my heart and His plan for us."

Elkhana took her into his arms and kissed her. "I know that these have been trying times for you. But don't forget that we have Sarah and Rebekah as our examples. In due time Hashem did visit them and they had sons. Don't lose heart, my love. For some, this takes longer than others. We will keep praying and trying." But days turned into weeks, months turned into years. Hannah continued to pray and cry out to G-D for answers. But it seemed her prayers fell on deaf ears.

EIGHT YEARS

Hannah and Elkhana celebrated their eighth year as husband and wife. Dinah and Nathan, along with their ten children, filled up the house with joy and laughter. Judith and Elkhana's siblings were also among the guests.

Hannah, again feeling the same old feelings that something was missing, went about the celebration with a fake smile and accolades. She adored her nieces and nephews! She was absolutely head over heels in love with them to be exact. She doted on them, but she just wasn't able to rid herself of the emptiness within her own soul. Elkhana, who was now also starting to worry that he wouldn't have an heir, was still good and kind to Hannah. He felt that his life was just as happy without children as with them and he didn't pressure her or speak unkindly to her for her inability to produce a child.

He was a good husband and hadn't spoken of putting her away for another woman, but he knew his wife was not happy with their situation. No matter how he tried to comfort her, she just refused to be comforted.

"Hannah," he would say, "Am I not better to you than ten sons?" Hannah would nod and smile at his words, but deep down she knew that having a child of her own was the one thing that would truly bring her happiness. She longed to hold a baby in her arms, to watch them grow and learn, and to experience the joys and challenges of motherhood. But as each year passed without a child, her hope began to fade.

As the celebration continued, Hannah excused herself from her guests and went for a walk. Dinah saw her leave and knew something was bothering her, so she went to find her. Hannah was walking and talking to herself as her sister approached, and Dinah fell in step alongside Hannah.

"I saw you leave," she said, "And you looked upset." Concern etched her face. Hannah turned to her sister, tears streaming down her face.

"I can't do this anymore," she said, her voice choked with emotion. "I can't pretend to be happy when I'm not. I can't keep putting on a brave face while my heart is breaking. Why won't Elohim bless me with a child? What have I done wrong?"

Dinah wrapped her arms around her sister, holding her tight. "You've done nothing wrong, Hannah," she said soothingly. "He has a plan for you, and maybe it's not what you expected. But you must have faith that He knows what's best for you."

Hannah sniffled, wiping her tears with her sleeve. "But how can I have faith when I feel so alone in my struggle?"

Dinah smiled gently. "You're not alone, Hannah. You have me, and especially Elkhana. And you have Hashem, who loves you more than anything. Even when we don't understand His way, we have to lean into Him, He will make straight your path."[25]

Hannah nodded, "Thank you, Dinah," she whispered. Dinah hugged her sister again. "I love you, Hannah," she said. "And I'm here for you, no matter what."

How had her baby sister become such a wise woman? She knew that Dinah had grown up fast after their father and mother had died. She faced her own trials and tribulations of being unwed and alone, and through them, she gained wisdom and strength. She had learned to rely on G-D for guidance and support, and her experiences had given her a perspective that allowed her to empathize with others, even when she didn't fully understand their pain. Her sister was a prime example of how G-D makes beauty from ashes.

For Hannah, her sister's presence was a source of strength and comfort, a reminder that she was not alone in her struggles and that G-D had a plan for her life, even if it wasn't the one she had envisioned for herself. "For I know the plans I have for you," declares the L-rd, "plans to prosper you and not to harm you, plans to give you hope and a future."[26]

Hannah said out loud while holding her sister's hand. "Yes, that's it! We don't know what He knows. And we can't even imagine what He has planned for us."

Dinah encouraged. "Stay the course sister, you'll see your blessing soon."

Hannah smiled weakly, she knew that what her sister said was the truth but she was losing her faith to actually see it. "Thank you, sister," she said. "I don't know what I would do without you."

Dinah smiled back at her. "You don't have to worry about that," she said. "I'll always be here for you." The sisters hugged each other, feeling a sense of peace and love wash over them. As they walked back to the celebration, Hannah felt a newfound sense of strength and hope, knowing that she had her family's love and support, and most importantly, the love and guidance of G-D.

Elkhana was waiting for her when she and her sister Dinah returned home. "There you two are!" He said. "Everyone is leaving and they are waiting for you to say their goodbyes." He could tell his wife had been crying and his own heart felt heavy as well.

He approached her and wrapped his arms around her. "Are you okay, my love?" he asked softly. Hannah leaned into his embrace, taking comfort in his warmth.

"I will be," she said, her voice barely above a whisper. "Thank you for being here for me."

Elkhana kissed her. "Always," he said. "I may not be able to take away your pain, but I can be here to support you through it."

Hannah looked up at him, tears in her eyes. "I don't know what I'd do without you," she said.

Elkhana smiled. "You don't have to find out," he said. "We're in this together, Hannah." Dinah smiled at the couple, feeling grateful for the love that they shared. She hugged them both saying goodbye, heading out with her husband and their children.

As Hannah and Elkhana said their goodbyes to the last of their guests, Hannah felt a sense of relief wash over her. The celebration was over, and now she could focus on healing and finding a way forward.

"Thank you for being so kind to everyone," Elkhana said, taking her hand.

"You always make everyone feel so loved and welcome."

She smiled, grateful for the distraction of the celebration. "It was my pleasure, I just wish…" she trailed off, unable to finish her sentence.

Elkhana squeezed her hand. "I know," he said. "But we'll get through this together." She nodded, feeling validated. Maybe there was a way forward, a path that she couldn't yet see. And with Elkhana by her side, she knew she could face whatever lay ahead.

Elkhana knew his wife desperately wanted a child and his own prayers weren't being heard. He didn't understand why; his heart too longed for a child and by the law of the land he needed children to secure his own name otherwise, his legacy would pass away.

"Like arrows in the hands of a warrior are children born in one's youth. Blessed is the man whose quiver is full of them. They will not be put to shame when they contend with their opponents in court."[27] He whispered to himself, but he felt like time was slipping away: as he was no longer young. He was nearing his forty-fourth year. Most men his age had a quiver full of children, and some even had a passel of grandchildren by now!

Elkhana was starting to feel the pressure of time on his own life and so the next day he went to the prominent teachers in his synagogue to inquire what the law said regarding his being without a son to carry on his name. Surely there was a way to secure his legacy.

As Elkhana sat with Yosef and explained his situation, Yosef opened the Torah and began to read some passages to Elkhana to comfort as well as support him. He read from the scrolls, "Remember how the L-rd your G-D led you all the way in the wilderness these forty years, to humble and test you in order to know what was in your heart, whether or not you would keep his commands."[28] Also, "G-D blessed them and said to them, "Be fruitful and increase in number; fill the earth and subdue it. Rule over the fish in the sea and the birds in the sky and over every living creature that moves on the ground." [29]

Lastly, he read, "Isaac prayed to the L-rd on behalf of his wife, because she was childless. The L-rd answered his prayer and his wife Rebekah became pregnant."[30] "Have you prayed over your wife Elkhana?" Yosef inquired.

To Elkhana's own shame he realized that while he was ministering to everyone else, he had failed to minister to his wife! "I've been a foolish husband Yosef," he lamented. And so Yosef encouraged him to pray fervently, with fasting, over Hannah. Then he told Elkhana that if in two years they still didn't have a child, Elkhana could return and they would discuss what Elkhana's next steps were in order to secure his lineage.

THE PRAYER OF A RIGHTEOUS MAN

Elkhana began a two-week fast for Hannah. He told her that he was not going to accept any food during this time while he afflicted his soul for their future children. Hannah joined her husband in this quest of petitioning the L-rd of hosts. They prayed and cried and their love for one another grew deeper. This was a very special time for Hannah. Surely now the L-rd would hear her heart's cry!

She felt grateful to Elkhana that he was also supportive after so many years of feeling alone. After the two weeks had concluded, Elkhana and Hanna waited for their answer. She was diligent to time her cycles and to be with Elkhana on the days when she was sure that she was ovulating, but one month turned into two, and then six.

Elkhana began to fast and pray again. He sat in sackcloth and poured his soul out to his creator. Hannah didn't join this new fast, but she still prayed. Her faith and her hope kept her from falling into utter despair, but she did feel like G-D wasn't listening. And so six months turned into a year and by the second year, Elkhana decided he needed to return to Yosef.

Yosef's home was a modest dwelling made of local stone and wood, situated on the outskirts of the village. A small garden with fruit trees and a vegetable patch surrounded the house. Inside, the main living area was spacious and airy with large windows that let in the sunlight. The walls were adorned with colorful tapestries and intricate patterns woven by Yosef's wife and daughters.

In the center of the room stood a sturdy wooden table, surrounded by several chairs. On the table were stacks of scrolls, ink pots, and quills, all neatly arranged. Yosef sat at one end of the table, with Elkhana sitting across from him. A small oil lamp provided light, casting flickering shadows on the walls.

In the corner of the room, a fireplace crackled, sending warm flames dancing up the chimney. The faint smell of wood smoke mingled with the aroma of freshly baked bread and roasting meat, indicating that Yosef's wife was preparing a meal in the adjacent kitchen. Overall, Yosef's home was simple but comfortable, a reflection of his humble character and devotion to the law.

"I don't know what I've done wrong," Elkhana cried openly. "I assume that the prayer of a righteous man is powerful and effective, so I must conclude that I am not righteous or worthy of Hashem's goodness!" Yosef looked at Elkhana with compassion and he prayed silently before he continued to speak for he saw before him a broken man. A man who was conflicted and losing faith.

Yosef spoke with careful consideration. "Elkhana I will admit that I had also expected Hashem to bless you and your bride with many children by now and I am at a loss for words. But look at the great witnesses before us in the Torah. Trusting is being confident of what we hope for, and being convinced about things we do not see. It was for this that Scripture attested the merit of the people of old. By trusting, we understand that the universe was created through the spoken word of Hashem so that what is seen did not come into being out of existing phenomena. By trusting, Able offered a greater sacrifice than Cain did; because of this, he was attested as righteous, with G-D giving him this testimony on the ground of his gifts. Through having trusted, he continues to speak, even though he is dead.

By trusting, Enoch was taken away from this life without seeing death — He was not to be found, because G-D took him away — for he has been attested as having been, before being taken away, well pleasing to G-D. Moreover, without trust, it is impossible to be well pleasing to G-D, because whoever approaches him must trust that he does exist and that he becomes a rewarder to those who seek him out.

By trusting, Noah, after receiving a divine warning about things as yet unseen, was filled with holy fear and built an ark to save his household. Through this trusting, he put the world under condemnation and received the righteousness that comes from trusting. By trusting, Abraham obeyed, after being called to go out to a place that HaShem would give him as a possession; indeed, he went out without knowing where he was going.

By trusting, he lived as a temporary resident in the Land of the Promise, as if it were not his, staying in tents with Isaac and Jacob, who were to receive what was promised along with him. For he was looking forward to a city with permanent foundations, of which the architect and builder is HaShem. By trusting, he received potency to father a child, even when he was past the age for it, as was Sarah herself; because he regarded the One who had made the promise as trustworthy. Therefore this one man, who was virtually dead, fathered descendants as numerous as the stars in the sky, and as countless as the grains of the sand on the sea-shore."[31]

Elkhana listened to Yosef and then interjected still in tears, "But haven't I shown my faith in this matter?"

Yosef replied, "With men it is impossible, but not with Hashem: for with Him, all things are possible. However, as it is written: What no eye has seen, what no ear has heard, and what no human mind has conceived" — the things HaShem has prepared for those who love him...[32] — he trailed off.

"Elkhana do you love Hashem?" Elkhana was taken aback by the question. "Yes...yes, I love him with all my heart soul, and strength!"

"Then," Yosef came back, "You are a righteous man."

The men sat in silence while Elkhana soaked in the words.

"You know," Yosef broke into the silence, "All these people kept on trusting until they died, without receiving what had been promised."

Elkhana thought about the words that Yosef spoke to him. "I don't believe that Hashem ever promised us a child Yosef, I just assumed that children came with the package. You know, um... it's just a part of marriage."

Yosef agreed and said "Yes, we are to be fruitful and multiply. It's just assumed that marriage will bring fruit. But I have known many couples who never did bear fruit. And you still have Torah to back up many stories of great heroes who had to wait a long time for children. I don't know why. I can't speak for Hashem. But we have the law and we have the prophets. And I've done my own research these last two years as I watched you both each Sabbath and Holy Days. I've found a place within our laws where you can take a second wife should your first wife fail to give you children."

The blood ran out of Elkhana's face! His head began to spin, and he felt faint! "I'm sorry Yosef... please forgive me. Did I miss understand you? He stammered. "Are you telling me I must give Hannah a certificate of divorce?!"

Yosef returned with empathy, "Yes, that's what I'm saying."

Elkhana jumped up from his seat; the chair crashed to the floor, "NO! No Yosef, no I can't! I won't! I wouldn't even consider it."

Yosef spread his hands to say the matter was closed. But Elkhana didn't concede, he asked another question. "You mentioned Abraham. He's our father, and he was righteous. He took Hagar as a wife to provide for his lineage. He didn't divorce Sarah. Why couldn't I take a second wife but not divorce Hannah?"

Yosef was now the one to be in complete shock. He opened his mouth and closed it. He didn't know what to say. "It's definitely forbidden..." He cleared his throat, "We don't practice polygamy now. Where it might have been necessary for the past, I'm very certain that Hashem didn't create man to have multiple wives!"

"But am I going to be shunned and cast out of the community if I did take a second wife?" Elkhana interrupted, pleading in his voice. Yosef didn't know what to say. He told Elkhana to pray on this matter and that he would talk with the other Torah teachers.

"But," Yosef concluded, "You have to also realize that even where the Torah is silent on something, it doesn't mean that the deed or act is permissible." He paused, "You also have to look at it this way, as we have seen in Torah, that bringing in a second wife never really worked out in the end. There was always contention in the home. There is a reason why HaShem made them male and female, at the beginning, and said, for this reason, a man will leave his father and mother and be united to his wife, and the two will become one flesh. So they are no longer two, but one flesh. Therefore what G-D has joined together, let no one separate...,"^33

He paused again, "This is why we say in the Talmud that forty days before a baby is conceived, Heaven has already chosen their soul-mate and has proclaimed who they will marry. We believe that before their souls were sent to earth, their union was predestined in heaven. There are only two halves to this union,[34] otherwise, it becomes a chimera...a very grotesque and unnatural creature, I urge you to use caution!" And with that, Yosef concluded the meeting with the promise he would consult with the leading teacher of the law about Elkhana's request.

Elkhana nodded slowly, deep in thought. He knew that he couldn't just ignore the law and do what he wanted, but he also couldn't bear the thought of divorcing Hannah. He left Yosef's house with a heavy heart, unsure of what to do. As he walked home, he prayed for guidance and wisdom. He knew that the decision he made would affect not just him, but also Hannah and any potential children they might have in the future. He hoped that he would find a solution that would be in line with both the law and his own conscience.

He was at an impasse though. The law gave him the legal right to divorce Hannah and marry another woman. He could possibly have sons with a new wife, and secure his name, but he loved Hannah way too much to hurt her like that and he knew that it wasn't her fault in the matter. For whatever reason, her womb was closed. He had prayed fervently for her but the miracle never came, and HaShem was silent on this matter.

Normally Elkhana was the one giving counsel to others at the gate. He was the one who would discern the will of G-D in matters and convey them to those who sought wisdom and a word from the Most High, but HaShem was absolutely silent on this matter. Surely in His sovereignty, He had a reason, but He had hidden it from Elkhana and even Yosef.

No one could tell him that taking a second wife wasn't the will of HaShem, but, Elkhana knew deep in his heart that he couldn't go against the very words that HaShem spoke at the beginning of creation, that a man should leave his father and mother and be united to his wife, and the two will become one flesh. He couldn't ignore the fact that this was the way HaShem intended for marriage to be and that going against it would bring about disharmony and strife in his household. He decided to continue to pray and seek guidance, trusting that HaShem would reveal His will in due time. Elkhana knew that the right decision wouldn't be easy, but he knew that with faith and trust in

HaShem, he would find the right path.

As the weeks progressed, and the answer still remained hidden from Elkhana, he began to second guess G-D's word again. He would pray and wait, but the answer was still not clear. And so, when he was called back to Yosef's house to hear the council's decision, Elkhana already knew what he was going to do. He took a deep breath as he entered Yosef's house. He could feel his heart pounding in his chest as he waited to hear the council's decision. Yosef and the other Torah teachers were seated around a table, deep in discussion. When Elkhana entered the room, they all turned to face him. Yosef motioned for him to take a seat.

"Elkhana," Yosef began, "we have consulted with the leading teacher of the law, and we have come to a decision regarding your request." Elkhana nodded; steeling himself for the answer he already knew was coming.

THE RIVAL WIFE

Yosef called a meeting with the other leaders in the community. He was concerned that if Elkhana took a second wife, there would be backlash. He was also worried, as Elkhana was a prominent member of the Levitical order and a respected man at the gate, other men with less education or standing would see Elkhana's actions as something to emulate and it would set a precedent. So he needed to find out what the law said regarding polygamy, and if it was "Assur" (forbidden).

Yosef invited several devout rabbis who were well versed in the law as well as the Talmidei Chachamim (Torah scholars) who would be able to help him find the answer for Elkhana. He also invited the High Priest Eli and his two sons. The debate was heated and many of the men became very agitated that one of their very own fellow teachers of the law was about to step over the line and possibly put himself and his reputation in jeopardy.

A man named Zadock brought up the law from Moses and the book of the Priest, pertaining to marrying a rival wife, but no one could agree on that one. Phinehas who was one of several men to side with Elkhana said that this particular law was about marriage to two sisters. He also argued that Abraham, their forefather and the father of the Jewish people and a great prophet himself, had a second wife beside Sarah, as well as a concubine. Hophni, his brother also chimed in and said that Jacob, who did marry sisters, would not have had to marry both women; except that he was deceived. And in the end, he had four wives. And Esau, his brother, had three wives. But the High Priest, Eli, Hophni, and Phinehas' father interjected and reminded his sons that Esau was not a devout or righteous man. He had sold his birthright and was an idolater. "But father," Hophni interrupted, "Jacob was seen as more pious and obedient, and he did practice polygamy, so I think the answer is clear!" He threw his hands up.

In the end, the men all conceded the issue back to Yosef and told him he had to be the final judge on the issue. A few days later, Yosef called for Elkhana to visit him. And he informed him that the council had decided he was in the right to take a second wife, and not give Hannah a certificate of divorce. But, he warned Elkhana, he had to follow the ketubah that he and Hannah had signed and that she also had to give her consent to him marrying another woman. He also reiterated to him that he still didn't agree with this arrangement, as in every Torah reading, where there are two or more women, there was always a rivalry.

Sarah despised Hagar and had her cast out. Ishmael and Isaac's offspring still had a conflict to that day! Leah and Rachel were rivals, which led to their children fighting, and they mistreated Joseph selling him as a slave. "Nothing good ever comes from this kind of arrangement," he warned Elkhana. "I advise you to seriously take my words to heart," he concluded. "May Hashem judge me blameless in your decision, should you choose not to heed my warning".

With that information, Elkhana set out for home. His heart was a mix of emotions. He loved Hannah! He would die for her. But he needed his name to be preserved in the land of the living before he did die!

"How will I tell her?" He thought to himself. But when he arrived home, he had to put the matter out of his mind because Aaron and Abigail; Peninnah's parents were visiting. It was an unexpected visit. They had not seen one another for some time. Peninnah was now a beautiful young woman. No longer the rambunctious eight-year-old child they had walked to Shiloh with on the pilgrimage so many years before. The table was set for five and everyone was sitting and waiting on Elkhana. And so he washed his feet quickly at the door and rinsed his hands, then sat down.

All eyes were on him. He said the blessing and they began to eat, but little did he know that he had been the subject of discussion for the last hour. And, so after the meal, he wasn't ready for what Hannah proposed to him. But once he heard it, his heart stopped beating for half a second and he became pale. His face must have shown it or he must have swayed and almost fallen out of his seat; because soon Hannah was beside him patting his hand in concern.

"Elkhana, are you OK?" Hannah asked, pouring him a glass of water. Elkhana looked at Hannah but it seemed he was looking through her. His mind did not comprehend her words. Aaron saw the confusion in his friend's eyes, cleared his throat, and said: "Let's give Hannah and Elkhana some time to talk. We will take a walk." And with that, he got up and left the house. Abigail and Peninnah close at his heels.

Once the door closed Elkhana felt like he could breathe again, but he still looked at his beautiful wife with a confused expression. "I don't know what to say, Hannah!" He said quietly. "I just don't know..."

"My love," Hannah broke in, "This has to be the answer! We have prayed and given this matter to Hashem. And I've prayed for many more years than you. But still, the Most High hasn't seen fit to answer either one of us. I thought surely your prayers would absolutely reach Heaven!" She exclaimed. "But in His sovereignty, He had chosen to remain silent on this. We can't keep putting this off. We have to act now! I am asking you to marry Peninnah! I'm a barren woman and the law is clear where I am concerned. You must have children, and I can't give you any." She said, choking back a sob.

Elkhana hugged his wife. "Okay, my love," he agreed. "I'll take Peninnah as my wife, but only for the sake of bearing my children. Moreover, I will not give you a divorce either! You are my light! It's you that I love. I want you to know that I talked to Yosef today about the law concerning your barrenness, and he did tell me at first I would have to divorce you to preserve my lineage..., Hannah I rejected his words!" He finished.

Hannah nodded through the tears streaming down her face. "I know, Elkhana. I knew you were meeting with him, and I knew about the council meeting. One of my friends is married to a man who was a part of the meeting and she told me that you had asked for them to decide what is lawful. I knew you loved me, I did not know how much until she told me you were about to risk your reputation for me! I love you too, and I trust that this is the right decision. It's not easy, but it's necessary. I didn't want you to feel alone in this decision. And we will get through this together."

Elkhana held her close, feeling a mixture of guilt and gratitude. Guilt for not being able to give Hannah the child she so desperately wanted, and gratitude for her selflessness and understanding. He knew he had a lot to think about, but for now, he just wanted to hold his wife and reassure her that they would face whatever challenges lay ahead as a team.

As they sat together in silence, Elkhana thought about the weight of his decision. He knew that taking Peninnah as his wife would not be easy. There would be challenges and obstacles to overcome. But he also knew that it was the only way to fulfill his duty as a husband and father. He would have to learn to love Peninnah and treat her with the same kindness and respect that he showed Hannah.

Meanwhile, Hannah, still in her husband's embrace, felt a mixture of emotions. She was relieved that Elkhana had agreed to her request, but at the same time, she couldn't help but feel a sense of sadness and betrayal. The thought of her husband being intimate with another woman was almost too much to bear, but she knew that she had to be strong and supportive for the sake of their marriage and family. As they sat together in silence, both in their thoughts and emotions, they knew that their lives were about to change forever. But they also knew that they had each other, and that was all that mattered.

Elkhana called back Aaron and told him that he would accept his daughter as his wife. They exchanged their sandals and the deal was struck. Abigail and Peninnah stood back with tears in their eyes on one side of the room, while Hannah stood on the opposite side, leaning against a wall for support, all alone. Her own grief flowed down her face.

THE SECOND WEDDING

The wedding day for Elkhana and Peninnah was arranged and preparations began. Aaron, along with several men in the community, helped Elkhana build Peninnah's house. The love and time that Elkhana had put into Hannah's home were not incorporated into this structure, but it was sturdy and would be sufficient for her needs.

Hannah felt a sense of dread and sadness as the day of the wedding drew closer. She couldn't shake the feeling that this was a mistake and that she was losing a part of herself, but she tried to push those feelings aside and focus on supporting Elkhana and Peninnah.

Her sister, Dinah, was upset about the whole situation and pleaded with Hannah to reconsider the idea of Elkhana taking another wife. She knew how much her sister loved her husband and didn't want to see her suffer through this. "Hannah, I understand how much you want a child, but this isn't the answer. You don't have to share your husband with someone else just to have a child. There must be another way," Hannah listened to her sister's words, but she couldn't see any other solution. "Dinah, I appreciate your concern, but I have thought about this long and hard. This is the only way for Elkhana to have a child and the family he deserves," Hannah replied, feeling conflicted.

Dinah sighed, knowing she couldn't change her sister's mind. "Just promise me you'll take care of yourself and that you'll talk to me if things become too difficult," she said, hugging Hannah.

Hannah nodded, grateful for her sister's support. "I promise, Thank you for always being there for me," she said, wiping away a tear.

Judith, Elkhana's mother was also against this unusual union. She loved Hannah as a daughter. She had also prayed for her and her son to have children. She knew how much Hannah had struggled over the last ten years and she didn't want to see Hannah in more pain. Her heart was breaking so much that it made her very sick. She approached her son a few weeks before the wedding, begging him to call it off.

"You just can't go through with this son!" She cried. "You are an honorable man, respected at the gates. You will be shunned." She covered her face, tears falling to the ground. "Poor Hannah! She's had so much pain in her life. This will not be healthy for either one of you!" Elkhana was taken aback by his mother's sudden outburst. He had always respected her opinion and valued her advice, but this time he knew she couldn't change his mind.

"Mother, I know this is not what you wanted for Hannah or me, but we must accept our reality. We have prayed for a child for so long, and it seems like Hashem has not answered our prayers. Peninnah will give me children, and I cannot ignore my duty as a husband and a father. I will still love and cherish Hannah as my wife, but I have to take Peninnah as my second wife for the sake of our lineage."

Judith could see the pain in her son's eyes. She knew he had made up his mind. She reluctantly nodded and hugged him tightly, hoping that somehow everything would work out for the best. She didn't know if she could accept Peninnah as her daughter-in-law and love her as much as she did Hannah, but she promised her son that she would try to support them.

On the day of the wedding, Hannah watched from a distance with tears in her eyes. Dinah and Leah were at her side for support, as Elkhana and Peninnah exchanged vows and became husband and wife. Hannah tried to push aside her feelings of jealousy and sadness, reminding herself that this was a sacrifice she had chosen to make for the sake of Elkhana having a child and preserving his name in the land. She focused on her faith and the belief that G-D had a plan for her life, even if it was not what she had hoped for or expected.

As Elkhana signed the ketubah with his new bride, he could not help but think about his first wedding. It was a much happier day for him. Although today was filled with joy from the bride next to him, and her ecstatic parents, along with the merry guests all around him, Elkhana couldn't help but feel like this wasn't right. He didn't love Peninnah, though she was extremely attractive. His heart was broken for Hannah who watched them at a distance and he looked at her while he put the veil over Peninnah's face.

Elkhana walked with his mother to the Chuppah. Things were changing quickly and he wasn't able to stop it. As the wedding celebrations continued, Elkhana couldn't shake off the feeling of guilt and sorrow. He knew he had hurt Hannah deeply by marrying Peninnah, even though it was for the sake of having children, and at her suggestion. He wished that he could turn back time and change things. That was impossible now. Elkhana made a vow to himself that he would do everything in his power to make sure that Hannah knew she was loved and cherished, even if he had to go against societal norms to do so.

During the wedding celebration, Hannah felt a deep sense of loneliness and isolation. She tried to distract herself by spending time with Leah and her children, but she found herself crying often and feeling lost and confused about her future.

As she sat alone in her home, Hannah prayed to G-D, pouring out her heart and asking for guidance and comfort. She felt a sense of peace wash over her as she remembered the words of the prophet Isaiah, "Fear not, for I am with you; be not dismayed, for I am your G-D; I will strengthen you, I will help you, I will uphold you with my righteous right hand."[35] Hannah knew that G-D was with her, and she felt a renewed sense of strength and hope. She resolved to be strong for Elkhana and to support him in his marriage to Peninnah, even though it was difficult for her.

Over the next few weeks, she watched as Elkhana and Peninnah settled into their new life together. She tried to be happy for them, but her heart still ached. She continued to pray to G-D for a miracle, knowing that nothing was impossible for Him.

Despite the challenges and pain that she faced, Hannah remained faithful and hopeful. She knew that G-D had a plan for her life, and she trusted that His plan would ultimately lead to her happiness and fulfillment.

As the days turned into weeks and months, Elkhana tried his best to balance his duties as a husband to both Hannah and Peninnah. It was not an easy task, and he often found himself struggling to find time for both of them. He noticed that Hannah seemed more distant and quieter than usual, and it broke his heart to see her in pain.

One day, Elkhana decided to take Hannah on a walk to a nearby field. It was something they used to do before Peninnah came into the picture, and he hoped it would help them reconnect. As they walked, Elkhana held Hannah's hand tightly and spoke softly to her, telling her how much he loved and cherished her. Hannah listened but did not respond, as her heart was heavy.

Elkhana noticed Hannah's sadness and stopped walking. He turned to face her and gently lifted her chin to look into her eyes. "Hannah, my love, what is troubling you?" he asked with concern in his voice.

Hannah hesitated for a moment before finally speaking. "I know that this is the agreement we made together. I knew it wasn't going to be easy. I was not deceiving myself in the least when I imagined you with Peninnah. But now we are on this journey and it's just hard! I hope that I do not sound selfish, but sometimes I find myself regretting this decision."

Elkhana looked at Hannah with understanding and empathy. He squeezed her hand gently and said, "I know this is not easy for you. But please know that I love you and that will never change. You are the one who holds the key to my heart, and nothing and no one can change that." Hannah felt a sense of relief wash over her as she listened to Elkhana's words. She knew deep down that he loved her, but hearing him say it out loud made all the difference.

"Thank you," she said, a small smile forming on her lips. "Your words mean everything to me."

They stood there for a moment, just looking into each other's eyes. At that moment, all the pain and uncertainty seemed to melt away, and they were left with a deep sense of love and connection.

Over time, Elkhana grew to appreciate Peninnah's beauty and her kind heart. She was a good wife to him, and he tried his best to be a good husband to her. However, he could not truly give her his heart, because it belonged to Hannah. He would often find himself lost in thought, wondering what could have been if only things had gone differently.

Peninnah knew that she was the second choice. She saw how Elkhana devoted himself to Hannah. He gave her a double portion of everything that he had. He did take care of Peninnah, but she knew that she was not favored or loved. This was a hard trade-off. Her parents had fallen into financial hardship and they had gone to Hannah offering Peninnah as a servant so that their child would be taken care of. It was Hannah who suggested that she marry Elkhana instead and her parents were just as pleased with that set of arrangements over their daughter being a servant. Now she was married to a man four times her age, her only role in the marriage was to produce offspring. Her purpose in life was bleak. She wasn't loved, and she had no real prospects other than to provide heirs for Elkhana, but maybe once she did give him the children he desired his heart would soften towards her and eventually even love her.

Four months after their wedding Peninnah told Elkhana that she was with child. His face lit up with the news and he kissed her passionately. Peninnah felt her circumstances about to change for the better.

Hannah was a mixture of emotions at the news that Peninnah was pregnant so soon after she and Elkhana were married. Even though it was her idea for the union, she didn't consider what the ramifications to her own mental health would be like.

As happy as she was for Elkhana finally being able to have a child, the news brought her infertility back to the forefront of her mind. She couldn't help but feel jealous and resentful towards Peninnah, despite knowing that it wasn't her fault. Hannah tried to push these negative emotions aside and focus on being a good wife and supporting her husband through this joyous time, but it was a difficult task. She found herself withdrawing from social situations and spending more time alone, often weeping and praying to G-D for some kind of resolution to her situation.

Dinah saw the mental decline in her sister and she enlisted Leah's help in comforting Hannah. The two women would often visit Hannah, bringing her food and sitting with her, listening to her concerns and offering words of encouragement.

As much as Hannah struggled, Peninnah's pregnancy progressed smoothly and she gave birth to a healthy son whom they named Joel. Elkhana was overjoyed and couldn't stop beaming at the sight of his new son. But, while he was holding the baby, he noticed a sadness in Hannah's eyes. He knew that she was struggling and he felt guilty for causing her pain. He wanted to comfort her, he just didn't know how.

As the years passed, Peninnah gave birth to more children, while Hannah remained childless. As Peninnah's status grew with her children, she became arrogant and became a sore subject between the two women. Peninnah often taunted Hannah and made her feel inferior. Hannah tried to ignore her, but it was becoming increasingly difficult. She began to resent Elkhana for taking another wife. The situation was tearing her apart and she didn't know how much longer she could handle it.

PENINNAH

She had been a happy child. The only daughter of her parents, Aaron and Abigail,she was full of energy and didn't like to sit still for long. Peninnah had an inquisitive mind and she never met a stranger. She was outgoing and could befriend a stone, her mother would joke. They were proud of their daughter's intelligence and sociable nature.

Peninnah's curiosity led her to ask many questions about everything, and her parents did their best to answer them all. Her parents often marveled at her enthusiasm for life. She had a contagious spirit and could brighten anyone's day with her smile.

Her parents did their best to nurture her curiosity and zest for life. They knew they had something special in their daughter, and that she had a bright future ahead. Her father secured a prospective husband for her at only six years of age. The man she was promised to was twelve years her senior. He had many prospects and would be a prosperous merchant like his father, who traveled around selling spices and fine textiles. With their union, Peninnah's parents would be financially set for life.

But for now, she was allowed to just be a child and explore her world. She wasn't aware of the arrangement that her father had made for her. She was carefree and enjoyed spending time with her friends and family, going on adventures, and learning new things.

Peninnah was eight years old when she met Hannah on their pilgrimage to Shiloh and she instantly formed an attachment to the older woman. She would play games with Hannah and her nieces and nephews along the trail or make up silly stories. Her parents didn't wonder where she was, as long as she was with Hannah. They relished the break they got when she was visiting her friend and enjoyed the new freedom they had found when she was exploring the trails with the other children and Hannah.

Hannah introduced Peninnah to her husband, Elkhana. Peninnah was intrigued by the man and his gentle mannerisms. She observed how he treated Hannah with love and respect. It left a lasting impression on her.

The road to Shiloh was a long and arduous trek, but with Hannah's enthusiasm the journey wasn't as tedious. Peninnah cherished the extra attention and company. Hannah would often tell Peninnah stories about her childhood and her hopes for the future. She introduced Peninnah to her family when they stopped overnight during the journey for a respite. She showed her all of her favorite places to play, and the best trees to climb. Hannah took Peninnah and the other children to play at her favorite stream, where they waded barefoot in the cool water and caught fish for their supper. She encouraged Peninnah to pursue her passions and dreams, and the two developed a strong bond.

As they arrived in Shiloh, Hannah brought Peninnah with her to the market to buy the necessary foods for the festivities. Peninnah was full of wonder as she walked with Hannah from each booth. The bigger city was full of mystery and she asked a lot of questions. As Hannah walked with Peninnah, holding her hand, she told her about the history of the town as well as the reason for the celebration of Sukkot. They purchased fruits, vegetables, and other supplies for the week-long celebration, and made their way back to the temple to join the other worshipers.

Aaron and Abigail remained good friends with Elkhana and Hannah and they often visited one another over the years.

At home, her parents began to train her for the responsibilities of being a wife and mother. They taught her how to run a household, manage finances, and cook for a large family. They also made sure she had an education in basic reading, writing, and math, uncommon for girls at her time.

Peninnah enjoyed learning and taking on new challenges, but there was always a sense of pressure and expectation from her parents. She knew that her future was already planned out for her and that she had to fulfill her duty as a wife and bear children for her husband. Despite this, Peninnah wanted to have her dreams and aspirations too and she was sometimes stubborn about the plans her parents had made on her behalf, even though she knew it was pointless to argue with them about it. She did resent the idea of having to marry a man she did not know and might not ever love. His being wealthy only slightly piqued her interest, but it did help to know that she was going to move into a fine home and have beautiful clothing and other expensive things.

Then came financial struggles, and Peninnah's life took a downturn. The man she was betrothed to passed away suddenly and she had to put her dreams on hold and focus on survival. She became a pawn in her parents' plan to provide for thier future. At first the thought of being married off to another man she did not love frightened her but then her parents began to talk about her living as a servant in another household, and she began to cry and bemoan her situation.

She was beside herself at the thought of the demotion in her station, her own hopes and dreams were dashed to pieces, but then her mother suggested they talk to Hannah and ask if she needed help and if she would be willing to take Peninnah as a maidservant. Peninnah dried her tears, she liked that idea better. She and Hannah had always been good friends, and the arrangement really agreed with her. Maybe she would be able to pursue her own goals as Hannah's maid, and she could put off marriage for a few more years.

Peninnah had always wanted to be more than a wife and mother, though that was really all she prepared for. She wanted to explore her love of astronomy and math, but, she knew that women weren't allowed such pursuits in ancient Israel. She hoped that Hannah might be supportive of her passions, as she once encouraged her to go after her dreams when she was a child. She thought maybe she could just explore the idea. She hoped Hannah would be interested in learning too, at the very least she felt that Hannah would encourage her.

The fateful evening when Aaron, Abigail, and Peninnah called on Hannah, she was a jumble of nerves. She couldn't sit still as Aaron told Hannah what had befallen them, as they were now in debt and without Peninnah's marriage, they would be forced to sell her as a slave.

When Hannah had brought up the possibility that Peninnah could marry Elkhana, instead of being a servant, she was initially surprised by the proposal. In fact, she almost fainted from shock, but her spirits brightened and she was grateful to her friend who had not only opened her home to her but was also willing to share her husband too.

This wasn't a completely unusual situation. Though it was not a normal practice, she knew that these kinds of arrangements did occur. It would be somewhat awkward at first, but she loved Hannah and Elkhana. The idea of being married to Elkhana and potentially having children was now appealing to her. She had always secretly admired him. Peninnah knew that the situation was not ideal, but she was willing to do whatever it took to make the arrangement work. She hoped that with time, they could all learn to live together in peace and harmony.

But when Hannah told Elkhana the plan, he looked as if he was going to be sick. He was silent for so long that Peninnah thought her chance had been lost. To her surprise, he did accept the arrangement and her wedding day was a beautiful, joyful occasion. She was so very grateful that she had been rescued and redeemed by such a gentle and loving man.

Little did she know the struggles she would have to endure in her loveless marriage. Elkhana was very gentle and kind, and he was good to her but he didn't love her and she knew it. Now she was stuck in a nightmare where she was expected to play her part in Hannah's story. It was always about Hannah. Elkhana gave her the best of everything he had and Peninnah resented her for it. She had a nicer home and better choices of meat at dinner. Her clothes were even better.

Once she found out that she was pregnant she knew her life would get better. Elkhana had to love her now and soon she gave birth to their first child. However, Elkhana's love never came. He loved his child, but he couldn't bring himself to love her. Not in the same way that she saw him with Hannah. He didn't look at her with the same devotion. He did not linger with her when they had meals together. He did not stay the whole night with her. He always went back to Hannah.

She remained strong and determined to make the best of her situation, to provide for her children, and to find happiness in her own way, but it was not always easy.

In the beginning, when she would hear Hannah crying, it made her sad for her friend; she never realized the burden Hannah carried until after her son was born. After a while, when she realized her loveless situation, she would feel a twinge of satisfaction, knowing that even though she may not have Elkhana' s love, she at least had his children. She was a mother, and that was something Hannah couldn't have.

Both women were miserable in their own ways she thought to herself. "But I will never have to worry about being alone and not taken care of should something happen to Elkhana, I have my son who will care for me in my old age." She was smugly aware of her fortune.

Peninnah threw herself into being the best mother she could be. She doted on her children and took pride in their accomplishments. She made sure that they had the best education. Peninnah would brag to Hannah about their milestones. She knew that got under her skin and she relished in it. She savored seeing Hannah in pain because she was also in pain.

Peninnah's behavior was fueled by her insecurities and feelings of inadequacy. She was trying to assert her worth and value by putting Hannah down, who was loved and cherished by Elkhana despite not having children of her own. Peninnah felt that Hannah was a threat to her position in the family, so she tried to diminish Hannah's worth in any way she could. However, this behavior was not justified, and it only served to create more tension and unhappiness in the household.

Elkhana loved his children dearly and made sure they had everything they needed. He was a kind and generous father who worked hard to provide for his family. However, he was not very involved in the day-to-day activities of his household, leaving Peninnah to take care of everything. He was often with Hannah at her home, oblivious to the strained relationship between his two wives, which caused even more tension in the household. Despite this, Elkhana remained a loving father to his children and a dutiful husband to Hannah whom he gave the double portion of everything.

A QUIVER FULL

Peninnah and Elkhana celebrated their seventh wedding anniversary. While it should have been a happy occasion, filled with laughter, music, and the warmth of family and friends, for Elkhana, the celebration was tinged with sadness. His mother Judith had passed away just a few months before, leaving a void that he couldn't seem to fill. Although Peninnah had given him several children by this time, a quiver full, he couldn't shake the feeling that something was missing.

Judith had always been a central figure in the family, doting on her grand-children and supporting her son and daughters-in-law. In time, she accepted Peninnah, even growing to love her too. But Elkhana knew that his mother always carried a burden with her. Despite Peninnah's efforts to be kind and respectful, Judith had always harbored a sense of unease around her.

With Hannah's struggles to conceive and bear children, the tension between the two women had only grown. Her love and devotion to her grandchildren eased it some, but Judith wasn't ever the same after her son married Peninnah. She would often be seen with Hannah, giving her encouragement and lifting her up in prayer. Her health began to deteriorate soon after Peninnah became part of her family. The heartache she felt for her son and Hannah took its toll on her physically, and she began to experience spells of dropsy.

Judith didn't begrudge Peninnah, she understood that she was just a pawn in the whole mess, and so, she took her under her wing as well. She made it a point to help Peninnah with the children until her health prevented it. Judith had also been a source of comfort and guidance for Elkhana.

In the months leading up to her death, she had urged him to be kinder and more loving to Peninnah, to see her as more than just a means to an end. Elkhana had struggled to follow her advice, but he knew deep down that she was right. In this way, Elkhana's heart for Peninnah did soften considerably. Peninnah knew that Judith was the reason for Elkhana's improvement, and so her presence was missed this night by both Elkhana and Peninnah.

As the evening wore on and the festivities continued, Elkhana felt increasingly hollow inside. He slipped away from the crowd and stepped outside, gazing up at the stars and praying for guidance. He knew that his situation was complicated, that his love for Hannah and his duty to Peninnah were in conflict. But at that moment, all he could feel was the weight of his mother's absence, the sense that things would never be quite right again.

It was then that he felt a hand on his shoulder. He turned to see Hannah standing beside him, her eyes filled with understanding. Without a word, they stood together in silence, watching the stars and feeling the cool breeze on their faces. After a while, Elkhana broke the silence and said, "It's hard to believe that my mother is gone. She was such a kind and loving person."

"Yes, she was," Hannah replied. "I will miss her so much. She was like a mother to me."

"I know," Elkhana said as he wrapped his arms around Hannah's waist. "And she loved you like her own daughter. She always talked about how proud she was of you and how much she wanted you to be happy."

"I will never forget how she encouraged me to keep praying and believing that HaShem would give us a child. She was always there for me, even when I felt like giving up." Hannah said, choking back tears now. " She never gave up hope either, Elkhana, your mother always had faith that she would see us with a child."

Elkhana replied: "My mother had a strong faith in the Most High. She believed that He had a plan for our lives, even when things seemed hopeless. I wish I had her faith. I feel that I let her down!"

"I know, me too," Hannah said. "I believed her faith so much, and what she told me about seeing the goodness of Hashem in the land of the living. But it's hard to wait, especially when we see others around us having children and being blessed in other ways."

"I understand how you feel," said Elkhana. "But we cannot compare ourselves to others. Hashem has a unique plan for each of our lives, and we must trust Him, even when we don't understand. For some reason, our story didn't include children. My mother never gave up that hope though."

"You're right," Hannah replied, "We must keep praying and trusting Him, just like Judith did. She would want us to have faith and hope, even in the midst of our sorrow. And I have not given up hope that one-day Jireh will see fit to give us a child, Elkhana."

"I will continue to pray and trust too, even when it feels like He's not listening," Elkhana resolved, looking up into the night sky. "I am grateful to have you by my side, Hannah." And he kissed her with a passion he had not felt in a long time.

Peninnah was watching the scene from her house. Her guests were preoccupied with the merriment of the evening. She had seen Elkhana leave the party and wanted to follow him until she saw Hannah with him. Her jealousy was piqued. Her mood was even more soured by the way she saw Elkhana kissing Hannah. Peninnah's feelings were a mix of jealousy and resentment. She felt a sense of competition with Hannah since marrying Elkhana, and the fact that he seemed to favor her only made things worse. She couldn't understand why he was so drawn to Hannah, especially since they had been unable to have children. Peninnah herself had borne several children, and she felt that this should make her the more favored wife.

As she watched them, Peninnah couldn't help but feel a sense of bitterness. She thought about her own children, and how they would carry on her legacy when she was gone. But what did Hannah have? Nothing! She was barren and would never be able to give Elkhana the children he so desperately wanted.

The sight of Elkhana and Hannah kissing only added fuel to Peninnah's fire. She could feel her anger rising, and she was tempted to storm over there and confront them, but she knew that would only make things worse. Instead, she turned away and went back into her house, seething with jealousy and frustration.

Deep down, Peninnah knew that her feelings were not rational. She knew that Hannah was a good person and that she didn't deserve to be hated but she couldn't help the way she felt. She was consumed by envy, and she didn't know how to get past it. It was like a weed that kept growing back each time she thought she had dealt with it, the weed of bitterness and strife would rear its ugly head once again.

That evening, after her guests had left, Peninnah sat alone in her room, her thoughts swirling with anger and resentment. She knew she needed to let go of these feelings, but she didn't know how. She tried to distract herself by focusing on her own blessings, her children, and her home, but the sight of Elkhana and Hannah together kept haunting her.

Suddenly, a thought crossed her mind. Maybe there was a way to turn this situation to her advantage. Maybe she could use Hannah's barrenness to her advantage, and make herself look better in Elkhana's eyes. She could emphasize her own fertility and show Elkhana that she was the better choice for him. It was a cruel and selfish thought, but Peninnah couldn't help it.

She got up from her chair and looked at herself in the mirror. She was still beautiful, despite her age and the stress of raising children. She could still make herself look attractive and alluring, and she could use that to her advantage. She would make sure that Elkhana noticed her more, that he saw her as a desirable woman, a woman who could give him more children. Peninnah knew it was a risky game to play. She could end up losing Elkhana altogether if he saw through her manipulations, but the temptation was too strong, and she was willing to take the risk. She took a deep breath and stepped out of her room, determined to win Elkhana's attention, and hopefully, his heart.

Hannah resumed her care of the widows in her village, she found solace in helping others and being kind and compassionate to those who were suffering. Her faith in G-D remained steadfast, despite the misery she felt at home due to Peninnah's constant torture. Elkhana seemed oblivious to it all. She regretted ever opening her mouth and uttering the fateful words that caused her this pain, but now there was nothing she could do about it.

Elkhana had married Peninnah at Hannah's behest. It was her fault. She thought that G-D would have taken special notice of her sacrifice, and taken pity on her as she now had a rival wife, just like Sarah. She expected G-D to be merciful to her because of her sacrifice,but He was silent in this. She couldn't understand why He would allow her to suffer so much, why He wouldn't grant her the one thing she had always wanted - a child of her own. She had prayed and fasted for years, made sacrifices, and yet in His sovereignty, He still did not answer her heart's cry. She felt like He was ignoring her pleas, which made her feel abandoned and alone.

Despite all of that, she continued to worship Him and remained faithful in her service to Him. "The L-rd is your refuge, Hannah, trust him."[36] Judith would tell her. "Lean into him daily to get your strength, but those who hope in Adonai will renew their strength, they will soar aloft as with eagles' wings; when they are running they won't grow weary, when they are walking they won't get tired."[37]

Judith had become a second mother to Hannah after Rachel passed away and so Hannah now felt she had lost her mother all over again. She missed her terribly. Her only solace was in helping others, in being kind and compassionate to those who were suffering. It gave her a sense of purpose, a reason to keep going. She knew that there were others out there who were hurting just like she was, and if she could help ease their pain in some way, it made her feel like her own suffering had some meaning.

Despite her efforts to keep a brave face, Hannah's infertility continued to haunt her. Every month, she hoped and prayed for a child, only to be left disappointed and heartbroken once again. She felt like a failure and believed that something was inherently wrong with her that prevented her from fulfilling her role as a wife and mother.

The pain of her home life was almost unbearable. Peninnah's constant taunts and jabs made her feel insignificant, and Elkhana did not seem to notice it, which added to her misery. Although he tried to be supportive, Elkhana didn't know how to ease her pain, and he often found Hannah in tears, pleading with G-D for a miracle.

Peninnah's jealousy towards Hannah grew as she saw the love and attention that Elkhana gave to her. Despite their unconventional marriage arrangement, Peninnah felt threatened by Hannah's presence in their home. She often made snide remarks and belittled Hannah in front of others, despite her initial excitement about sharing Elkhana with her.

Over time, Peninnah's insecurity and resentment grew, and she took her frustration out on Hannah, making their complicated situation even more difficult. As Elkhana distributed the offering among his sons, Peninnah would often speak up, trying to influence him to give more to her children. This behavior was not lost on Hannah, who felt a growing sense of frustration and anger toward her rival. It seemed like no matter how hard she tried, Peninnah always found a way to get under her skin.

But despite her efforts to provoke Hannah, Peninnah was also struggling with her own feelings of inadequacy. She knew that Elkhana loved her, but she could not help feeling jealous of Hannah's relationship with him. Every time she saw Hannah, with her kind and gentle demeanor, it only served to remind Peninnah of her own shortcomings.

Leah and Dinah knew that Hannah needed their support more than ever, especially with Peninnah's mistreatment of her. They offered words of encouragement and reminded her that she was loved and valued, even if she couldn't bear children. They also tried to confront Peninnah about her behavior, but it was difficult to reason with someone consumed by jealousy and bitterness.

Despite the difficulties, Hannah never lost faith in G-D. She continued to pray and ask Him for a child, even though it seemed impossible. She found comfort in the verse, "The L-rd brings death and makes alive; He brings down to the grave and raises up. The L-rd sends poverty and wealth; He humbles and He exalts."[38] Hannah often prayed, "El Roi, I am in a lonely place on my journey with you. But I know that you are the G-D who sees me. I have lived my life in your sight and served you with a grateful heart. Please show me your best."

THE PROMISE

Elkhana and Hannah traveled to Shiloh during their nineteenth year of marriage, to complete the annual sacrifice at the Tabernacle. Peninnah was heavy with child once again, and so she didn't make this journey with them. They enjoyed the time together alone, just as they had years before Peninnah became a part of their lives. As they arrived at the Tabernacle, they were filled with a sense of awe and reverence, knowing that they were in the presence of the Most High.

During the sacrifice, Hannah was moved to tears as she prayed silently to G-D, pouring out her heart to Him. She asked for forgiveness for her past jealousy and bitterness, and for His guidance and blessings in their future. Elkhana also prayed, thanking G-D for his wives and his children, and His continued grace and provision in their lives.

One day, after the sacrifice at Shiloh, Elkhana gave Hannah a double portion of the meal, but she wouldn't eat it. She got up, weeping, and went to pray. Eli the High Priest was sitting at his customary place beside the entrance of the Tabernacle. Hannah was in deep anguish, crying bitterly as she prayed, standing before Adonai.

She prayed silently "Master of the Universe! There is a heavenly host and an earthly one. The heavenly host neither eats nor drinks, are not fruitful and do not multiply, and do not die, but live forever. The earthly host eats and drinks, are fruitful and multiplies, and die. I do not know to which host I belong, whether to the heavenly host or the earthly one. If I am of the heavenly host, for I do not give birth, then I do not eat or drink, and I shall not die, but live forever. But if I am of the earthly host, let me then eat and drink, give birth, and die."[39]

She continued to pray, while standing in the temple with tears streaming down her face, slightly bending over as she poured her heart out. "Abraham did Your bidding, and You gave him a son when he was a hundred years old, while Ahab, who was a sinner and idolater, begot seventy sons! Sarah did Your bidding, and You gave her a son when she reached the age of ninety, while the wicked Jezebel bore seventy sons!"[40] And she made this vow: "O L-rd of Hosts, if you will look upon my sorrow and answer my prayer and give me a son, then I will give him back to you. He will be yours for his entire lifetime, and as a sign that he has been dedicated to the L-rd, his hair will never be cut."[41]

As she was praying to Adonai, Eli watched her. Seeing her lips moving but hearing no sound, he thought she had been drinking. "Must you come here drunk?" he demanded. "Throw away your wine!"

"Oh no, sir!" she replied. "I haven't been drinking wine or anything stronger, but I am very discouraged, and I was pouring out my heart to Elohim. Don't think I am a wicked woman! For I have been praying out of great anguish and sorrow."

"In that case," Eli said, "go in peace! May Adonai grant the request you have asked of Him."

"Oh, thank you, sir!"[42] she exclaimed. After her prayer, Hannah felt a sense of peace and comfort in her heart. She had poured out her deepest desires and fears to the L-rd and felt heard and understood. She no longer held bitterness towards Peninnah, as she had realized that her struggle was not with her rival, but with her fertility.

She went back and began to eat again, and she was no longer sad. Elkhana noticed that his wife seemed lighter and less burdened. He put his arms around her waist and kissed her. Hannah returned his embrace. The light had returned to her eyes.

The next morning they got up early and went to worship the L-rd once more. Then they returned home to Ephraim. On their journey back home, Elkhana slept with Hannah and HaShem remembered her.

Life went back to normal with Peninnah parading her heavy belly before Hannah. But now Hannah was different. She didn't hold any more bitterness in her heart.

One morning, when Peninnah went into labor she walked over to Hannah's house and asked her old rival for help. Her water had broken and Elkhana was at the gates. She had sent her eldest son Joel to fetch the midwife, but she was afraid that there wasn't time. And so Hannah helped Peninnah bring her daughter into the world. As she was cleaning the baby, the midwife arrived out of breath, but when she saw Hannah holding the baby girl, and Peninnah was being cared for; she looked at Hannah and said "Well done!"

Hannah beamed. She was overcome with many emotions, but none of them were of envy or bitterness. Hannah felt a deep sense of gratitude and joy for being able to help Peninnah in her time of need. She had prayed for a child for so long, and now she was able to assist in bringing a new life into the world. Hannah realized that her bitterness towards Peninnah had been replaced with compassion and kindness. She had let go of her jealousy and was able to appreciate the blessings in her life.

Nine months later, Hannah was also in labor. Her sister Dinah was with her. Elkhana was overjoyed at the sight of his son. They named him Samuel which means "Asked of G-D." HaShem had remembered Hannah at last!

The next year, Hannah didn't go with Elkhana and Peninnah to the annual sacrifice, after she had given birth to her son Samuel, instead, she stayed home with the child, saying that she wouldn't go until he was weaned and then she would take him to the Tabernacle and present him before the L-rd.

She wanted to fulfill the vow she made to G-D. It was a significant decision, as it meant that Hannah would only raise her son for three years, and then she would fully dedicate him to the service of the L-rd. Elkhana answered her, "Do what seems good to you; stay here until you have weaned him. May Adonai bring about what he said and help you keep your vow to Him."[43]

Peninnah was not as kind or helpful, she belittled Hannah and made her opinions known that she would never give Elkhana's children away. She would tell Hannah how unfair she was being to Elkhana and that she was a bad mother to even think about abandoning her long-awaited child, whom she cried for many years over; and, how could she even think about letting a stranger raise him?

But Hannah was faithful, and so when the day came and the child was weaned she made her way with Elkhana and Peninnah and their children, along with her own son Samuel. Her heart was heavy at the idea that she would be leaving him with Eli the priest. She knew that she would only see him once a year after she left him at the Tabernacle. But her vow to the L-rd held her steadfast to her task.

As they arrived at the Tabernacle, Hannah took Samuel and presented him before Eli. She told him, "Pardon me, my lord. As surely as you live, I am the woman who stood here beside you praying to the L-rd. I prayed for this child, and the L-rd has granted me what I asked of him. So now I give him to the L-rd. For his whole life, he will be given over to the L-rd."[44] And she worshiped the L-rd there.

Eli blessed Elkhana and Hannah and said, "May the L-rd give you children by this woman to take the place of the one she prayed for and gave to the L-rd."[45] Then they returned home to Ephraim.

Samuel grew up in the presence of the Adonai. Even as a young child, he ministered to the L-rd under the guidance of Eli the High Priest. Hannah had kept her vow to the L-rd and raised Samuel to be a man of G-D who would later become a great prophet in Israel.

Elkhana again slept with Hannah, and G-D had favor on her and opened her womb once more. On their twenty-third wedding anniversary, Hannah told Elkhana that she was expecting their second child. They worshiped the L-rd together, After so many long years of waiting, they were finally fruitful. The whole community was in awe over this miracle.

Leah stopped by Hannah's house to drop off a meal and let her know that her granddaughter, Rebekah, Hadassah's oldest daughter, was having her sixth birthday celebration. She was inviting Hannah, who had just given birth to her second baby, another boy, to the festivities

Hannah was grateful for Leah's visit and the meal she had brought. As they sat together, Leah shared some news from the village. She spoke of how the people were still talking about the miracle of Hannah's son, and how they had witnessed the power of G-D firsthand.

Hannah smiled, grateful for the reminder of G-D's faithfulness. She had been through so much in her life, but she had never lost sight of her faith. Leah's visit reminded her of the importance of community and the support of others.

As they continued to talk, Hannah couldn't help but remember the day that Rebekah was born. Hadassah had only recently married, and Leah was overjoyed at the thought of becoming a grandmother, all the while Hannah wasn't even a mother yet. The time had seemed to fly by from when Hadassah had been born to when she was having her own babies. And now Rebekah was growing up so quickly too, and Hannah was just starting. Her children would be playmates to Leah's grandchildren. It was so providential. Would she get to see her grandchildren, she wondered?

Samuel was now four years old, and living with Eli at the Temple. Leah saw the quick change in her friend's eyes and knew she was missing her son.

As Leah prepared to leave, she took Hannah's hand and looked deeply into her eyes. "Remember, Hashem has a plan for you and your family. His ways are not always our ways, but His love is constant and unfailing. Keep your eyes fixed on Him, and He will guide you through all that lies ahead."

Hannah felt a sense of peace wash over her as Leah spoke. She knew that the road ahead would not always be easy, but with G-D's help, and the support of her family and friends, she was ready to face whatever came her way.

Leah gave Hannah a warm embrace before leaving, and Hannah felt a sense of gratitude for her dear friend. As she watched Leah walk down the path, Hannah looked down at her sleeping son and silently prayed for his future.

She knew that she couldn't control what was to come, but she trusted G-D's plan for her and her family. And as she sat there, holding her newborn son, Hannah felt a renewed sense of hope and faith in the journey ahead.

"And G-D remembered Hannah and he gave her five more children; three sons and two daughters, because she was faithful and gave Him her firstborn son. Meanwhile, the boy Samuel grew up in the presence of the L-rd". 1 Samuel 2:21

THE END

Epilogue

As we conclude the journey of Hannah and her enduring faith, we reflect on her prayer as recounted in the Holy Bible 1 Samuel 2:1-10

2:1 "And Hannah prayed and said: "My heart rejoices in the L–rd; My [i]horn is exalted in the L–rd.[j]I smile at my enemies Because I rejoice in Your salvation. **2** "No one is holy like the L–rd, For *there is* none besides You, Nor *is there* any rock like our G–d. **3** "Talk no more so very proudly; Let no arrogance come from your mouth, For the L–rd *is* the G–d of knowledge; And by Him, actions are weighed. **4** "The bows of the mighty men *are* broken, And those who stumbled are girded with strength. **5** *Those who were* full have hired themselves out for bread, And the hungry have ceased *to hunger.* Even the barren has borne seven, And she who has many children has become feeble. **6** "The L–rd kills and makes alive; He brings down to the grave and brings up. **7** The L–rd makes poor and makes rich; He brings low and lifts up. **8** He raises the poor from the dust *And* lifts the beggar from the ash heap, To set *them* among princes And make them inherit the throne of glory."For the pillars of the earth *are* the L–rd's, And He has set the world upon them. **9** He will guard the feet of His saints, But the wicked shall be silent in darkness."For by strength, no man shall prevail. **10** The adversaries of the L–rd shall be broken in pieces; From heaven, He will thunder against them. The L–rd will judge the ends of the earth."He will give strength to His king, And exalt the [k]horn of His anointed."

1 Samuel 2:1-10 The Holy Bible

Afterword

* * *

Hannah's Hope: Finding Healing in Infertility

Introduction:

Welcome to Hannah's Hope, a Bible study page for women who have struggled with infertility. Just like Hannah in the Bible, many women throughout history have faced the pain and shame of not being able to conceive a child. But Hannah's story also offers hope and healing, as she turns to HaShem in prayer and eventually gives birth to a son who becomes a great prophet.

In this study, we will explore Hannah's story and its relevance to our own lives, as well as connect as a community of women supporting each other through this difficult journey.

Section 1: Historical and Cultural Context

In this section, we will explore the societal expectations and attitudes towards women in biblical times, as well as the cultural and religious significance of having children.

We will look at the practice of early marriage and betrothal in biblical times, and how this affected women's lives. Girls were often betrothed at a young age, sometimes as young as twelve years old, and married soon after reaching puberty. This was done to ensure that they could bear children while still in their prime childbearing years.

Being married at a young age affected women's lives significantly. For one, it meant that they had very limited opportunities for education or personal development outside of their roles as wives and mothers. They were expected to take on domestic responsibilities and bear children, often without any knowledge or preparation for these tasks. This could lead to a sense of isolation and dependence on their husbands and families.

In addition, marrying at a young age often meant that girls were not able to fully mature or develop their own identities before being thrust into the role of wife and mother. They may not have had the opportunity to explore their own interests, pursue education or career goals, or establish their own sense of independence.

Furthermore, marrying at a young age often meant that girls were at greater risk of complications during childbirth and other health issues related to early pregnancy and childbearing.

Overall, being married at a young age had significant effects on women's lives, limiting their opportunities and sense of agency while placing significant physical and emotional demands on them as wives and mothers.

In this portion, we will explore the limited opportunities for education and domestic roles that women had in ancient Israel, and how this impacted their value and worth.

Women in biblical times had limited opportunities for education and were often confined to domestic roles. They were expected to marry and have children, with their worth and value being tied to their ability to do so. Women were also subjected to laws and customs that favored men, such as the requirement for a man to provide a divorce document (a "get") in order for a woman to be legally divorced.

- Examine the laws and customs that favored men, such as divorce laws, and how this affected women's status and agency.

In Hannah's day, divorce was permitted under Jewish law, as outlined in the Torah (Deuteronomy 24:1-4). A man could divorce his wife if he found "some indecency" in her, which was interpreted to mean adultery or other serious sexual misconduct. The man was required to give his wife a written document, called a "get," which served as proof of the divorce and allowed her to remarry.

However, the process of divorce was primarily controlled by men, and women had limited rights in the matter. A man could divorce his wife without her consent, whereas a woman could only initiate divorce under certain circumstances, such as if her husband was unable to provide for her or if he was abusive.

Furthermore, divorced women were often stigmatized and had limited opportunities for remarriage, especially if they were older or had children. This made divorce a difficult and risky option for women, and many stayed in unhappy marriages because they had few other options.

- Reflect on the cultural and religious significance of having children in ancient Israel, and how infertility was viewed as a curse.

Firstly, in ancient Israel, children were seen as a gift from G–D and were highly valued. The continuation of the family line was considered very important, and having children was seen to ensure the family's legacy and honor. This was especially true for men, who needed sons to carry on the family name and inherit property.

As we see in Deuteronomy 25:5–6, which states: "If brothers dwell together, and one of them dies and has no son, the wife of the dead man shall not be married outside the family to a stranger. Her husband's brother shall go into her and take her as his wife and perform the duty of a husband's brother to her. And the first son whom she bears shall succeed to the name of his dead brother, that his name may not be blotted out of Israel." Women were also highly valued for their ability to bear children, as it was seen as their primary purpose in life.

Secondly, in ancient Israel, there was a belief that barrenness was a curse from G–D. If a woman was unable to have children, it was seen as a sign of divine displeasure and could lead to stigmatization and shame. This belief was based on the idea that G–D had promised to bless his people with many offspring, as outlined in the covenant with Abraham (Genesis 12:2–3). So, being unable to have children was seen as a failure to fulfill this promise and could lead to feelings of shame and inadequacy.

Thirdly, in ancient Israel, having children was seen as a way to secure one's future and provide for oneself in old age. There was no social security or retirement system in place, so having children was seen as a way to ensure that one would be taken care of in old age. This was especially true for women, who had limited opportunities for economic independence and were often dependent on their husbands or sons for support.

Today, while infertility is still a significant issue, the cultural and religious significance of having children has changed in many societies. Children are still seen as a blessing, but their value is no longer tied solely to their ability to carry on the family name or provide for their parents in old age. Women also have more opportunities for education and employment, which has changed the expectations placed on them with regard to childbearing.

Where Adoption as a formal process was not common in biblical times, as it is in modern times, there are instances in the Bible where adoption is mentioned or implied.

For example, the story of Moses is a well-known example of a child who was adopted into a new family. Moses was born into a Hebrew family, but due to Pharaoh's decree to kill all Hebrew baby boys, his mother placed him in a basket and sent him down the river. He was found by Pharaoh's daughter and adopted into her family. Later in life, Moses became the leader of the Israelites and played a significant role in the history of the Jewish people.

Another example is the story of Esther, who was orphaned at a young age and adopted by her cousin Mordecai. She later became queen of Persia and played a key role in saving the Jewish people from destruction.

And we see that Ruth and Naomi formed a family bond even though they were not biologically related.

So, while adoption was not as formalized as it is today, there were instances in which children were taken in and raised by individuals who were not their biological parents, often out of necessity or as an act of compassion.

In more modern days Adoption has become an acceptable alternative to having children, especially for infertile couples.

In many ways, the changes in societal attitudes toward children and infertility reflect broader social and cultural shifts, including changes in gender roles, family structures, and economic systems.

Section 2: Hannah's Story

In this section, we will delve into the story of Hannah in the Bible, looking at the challenges she faced and the ways in which she found hope and healing.

- Read and discuss the story of Hannah in 1 Samuel 1-2, focusing on the emotional and spiritual struggles she faced.
- Consider the significance of Hannah's prayer in 1 Samuel 1:10-20, and how she turned to G-D in her pain and longing.
- Explore the ways in which Hannah's story offers hope and healing to those struggling with infertility today, and the lessons we can learn from her faith and perseverance.

Section 3: Practical Applications

In this section, we will explore practical ways to apply the lessons we have learned from Hannah's story to our own lives, as well as connect with each other as a community of women.

Provided below are links to relevant resources, such as podcasts, videos, or websites, for further study and support.

```
https://youtu.be/NuG-Dc8mZVs
https://youtu.be/pNH5fOLYoPg
https://youtu.be/AOZunIRvF4A
https://youtu.be/5e1hxNT8WDs
https://youtu.be/0yJsin_SSj4
https://youtu.be/CIPihXDxpss
infertility - Risen Motherhood
Does Christianity have anything good to say to the infertile? |
```

```
Saltwater and Honey
https://podcasts.apple.com/us/podcast/grief-06-grief-in-adoption-an-
interview-with-jen-oshman/id1072833310?i=1000606436458
Music:
Take Courage, Bethel Music Kristene DiMarco
https://youtu.be/q9XNqEf8jF0
There Was Jesus Zach Williams
https://www.youtube.com/watch?v=x9w8yfOkUMM
```

Group Discussion:

This is a safe space to share your own thoughts and feelings.

- If you feel led, please share your own experiences and insights.
- What is your TTC journey and testimony?

1.How can we learn from Hannah's example of giving her emotions to G-D? What practical steps can we take to give our worries and fears to G-D

2.Why do you think Hannah still felt like something was missing even though she was happy with her family? How can we find true fulfillment in our lives?

3.How can difficult trials and challenges be seen as gifts from G-D in the process of refining one's soul?

4.In what way are you trusting in G-D's timing while you are struggling with unfulfilled desires?

5.What can we do to maintain hope and faith during difficult times?

6.Can you learn to trust in G-D's plan when things don't go according to your plans?

* * *

Faith Hope and Love:

In this section, we will briefly look at the difference between Hannah and Peninnah's faith and their actions in regard to their relationship with G–D:

Please answer these questions within the group:

1. What are the differences between Hannah and Peninnah? What are their motivations and attitudes toward each other?
2. How does Hannah's faith in G–D sustain her through her struggles with infertility and Peninnah's mistreatment?
3. How does Peninnah's lack of faith contribute to her behavior towards Hannah? How does this affect their relationship?
4. How does Judith's legacy impact the lives of Hannah and Peninnah? How do they respond to her legacy?
5. How can we apply the lessons learned from Hannah and Peninnah's story to our own lives, especially in regard to our faith and relationships with others?

* * *

Adoption:

In this section, we are going to talk about Adoption as an option to create your family. This is a very touchy and emotional subject because most people naturally want to have children of their own.

They want to look into their children's eyes and see their own eyes looking back. They want to say "Oh, he had your nose," or "Oh, she's got your ears," They want to see Grandpa Joe or Grandma Jean in their babies' faces.

With adoption, this isn't possible normally, unless you're adopting a biological family member. (Kinship adoption) The reason I am including this brief Bible study and making a case for adoption is because that is the path we choose for our family.

It's certainly not the path for everyone. You must know right out of the gate that adoption is a form of brokenness. A child is being taken from his biological family and placed into one that isn't theirs unless, again, they are in Kinship. And so, the brokenness you must accept is the loss of that child's biological family unit,and despite the circumstances, the loss of the biological parents. They too grieve for the child or children that they lost,no matter what the situation or reason for the separation.

It could be one where the birth mother was too young and decided to make the selfless decision to place her baby up for adoption where she chose the adoptive parents. It might be that CPS (Child Protective Services) had to remove the children and the parents weren't willing to work the services provided and their rights were terminated. Be it by choice or not,it doesn't matter!

The fact of the matter is, a child (children) no matter if they are newborn or toddler or even a teenager have been removed from their tree and placed in your tree. It's not natural,yet we see that HaShem's heart is for adoption. He shows us in many verses in his word where He takes an individual and adopts them,or He takes one tree and grafts it into another tree. The fruit will still be good. It's just placed into a better environment.

We can't dismiss adoption altogether. You must have a heart already for it though, and be willing to be broken. The term we use in foster care is that it's not all unicorns and rainbows. Foster children come with baggage,even if they are infants. They instinctively know they have been "abandoned" by their biological family. It's also very important to be honest about who they are and to tell them when they can understand the significance of their relationship to you,especially if you adopt interracially.

In today's Bible study, we will be looking at the story of Hannah and Samuel as an example of adoption in biblical times. We will examine how Hannah, who was barren and unable to have children, made the difficult decision to give her son Samuel to the L-rd by bringing him to the temple to serve under the high priest Eli. Through this act of surrender, Hannah essentially "adopted" Eli as a father figure for Samuel.

We will explore the emotions and challenges that Hannah may have faced in giving up her son and the unique relationship that formed between Eli and Samuel. Additionally, we will look at how the concept of adoption is reflected throughout the Bible and how HaShem's heart is for the fatherless and those in need of a family. We hope to gain a better understanding of adoption and how it can be a beautiful way to create a family, despite the brokenness that often accompanies it.

Group Discussion:

1.In what ways is Hannah's decision to give her child to the L-rd an act of adoption?

2.How does G-D's plan for Samuel's life demonstrate the value of adoption and the unique ways in which adopted children can serve His purposes?

3.What can we learn from Hannah's trust in G-D during the difficult decision to give up her child for adoption? How can this trust in G-D's plan apply to our own lives, particularly in situations related to adoption?

4.How does Eli's role in Samuel's life demonstrate the importance of community in the lives of adopted children? How can we better support families who have chosen to adopt?

5.How does the story of Hannah and Samuel illustrate G-D's heart for the vulnerable and marginalized, particularly children in need of a family?

6.What is our responsibility as Christians to care for these children and support families who are considering adoption?

Conclusion:

Adoption: Becoming Children of G-D

I. Review

- The concept of adoption as an option to create a family can be a touchy and emotional subject for many.
- Adoption is a form of brokenness that must be accepted, as a child is being taken from their biological family and placed into another family.
- G-D's heart is for adoption, and we can see this in several verses in the Bible.

II. Verse Study

- John 1:12-13: Those who receive and believe in Jesus are given the right to become children of G-D, born of G-D and not of human decision.
- Galatians 4:4-5: G-D sent his Son to redeem those under the law, that we might receive adoption to sonship.
- Romans 8:14-17: Those who are led by the Spirit of G-D are adopted as children and become heirs of G-D and co-heirs with Christ.
- 2 Corinthians 6:18: G-D declares that he will be a Father to us, and we will be his sons and daughters.
- James 1:27: True religion is to look after orphans and widows in their distress and to keep oneself from being polluted by the world.
- Deuteronomy 10:18: G-D defends the cause of the fatherless and the widow, and loves the foreigner among us.
- Mathew 25:40: Whatever we do for the least of Jesus' brothers and sisters, we do for him.
- Psalm 82:3: Defend the weak, the fatherless, the poor, and the oppressed.
- Psalm 68:5-6: G-D is a father to the fatherless, a defender of widows, and sets the lonely in families.

III. Group Discussion:

- What is the significance of being adopted as children of G-D?
- How does the act of adoption reflect G-D's character?
- In what ways can we care for orphans and widows, and how can we prevent being polluted by the world?
- How can we show love and care to those who are in need of a family or support system?
- Explain how adoption is a reflection of G-D's love and care for his children, and if this is true, are we called to care for the fatherless and the widow?
- By doing so, how are we showing love to Jesus himself and reflecting his character in the world?

Adoption Resources:
(1). NCFA (National Council For Adoption: Adoption Statistics -
National Council For Adoption (adoptioncouncil.org)
The 'snowflakes' we are referring to are frozen embryos. The term
'snowflakes' to describe frozen embryos was coined by an adoption
agency called Nightlight Christian Adoptions. Nightlight
facilitates many different adoption programs, including the
Snowflakes Embryo Adoption Program. Founded in 1997, the
Snowflakes program is considered the first embryo adoption program
in the world.
(2). Snowflakes Embryo Adoption & Donation (nightlight.org)
FOSTER CARE
In the United States, more than 407,000 children were in foster
care in 2020 -- the most recent year of data on record. The total
number of kids in care has decreased annually since 2017.
Foster care is a temporary living situation for children whose
parents cannot take care of them. While in care, children may live
with relatives, with foster families or in group facilities. There
are four ways children can leave foster care for permanent homes:
Reunification with birth parents or primary caregivers, adoption,
guardianship, and placement with relatives. Among children exiting
foster care each year, nearly half -- more than 107,000 kids in
2020 -- are reunited with a parent or primary caretaker.
https://www.aecf.org/topics/foster-care?

(3). www.AdoptUSKids.org (4). 11 Things To Know About International Adoption | Adoption.org (5). 7 Easy Countries To Adopt From - International Adoption

Thank you for joining us on this journey through Hannah's story. We hope that through studying her life and connecting with each other, you can find healing and hope in the midst of infertility. Let us continue to turn to HaShem in prayer and faith, knowing that He hears us and walks with us through every struggle and challenge.

3

A Personal Reflection on the Body and Faith

Unopposed

Estrogen Dominance, Progesterone Loss, and the Perimenopausal Body

For most of my reproductive life, my body gave warnings.

Breast tenderness.

Nipple sensitivity.

That familiar two-week signal before my period arrived.

They were never pleasant, but they were informative. They told me where I was in my cycle long before bleeding began. They told me ovulation had occurred. They told me progesterone was supposed to be rising, even when it never rose high enough to do its job.

Then perimenopause arrived, and the warnings disappeared.

Not suddenly. Not dramatically. Quietly.

My cycles stayed predictable. I didn't miss periods. But the internal contrast flattened. No ache. No tenderness. No warning. I only knew my period was coming because a Cycle Calendar App on my phone told me so.

That loss of symptoms did not mean balance.

It meant hormonal silence.

And in the body, silence often means depletion.

What Estrogen Dominance Actually Meant for Me

Estrogen dominance is one of the most misunderstood phrases in women's health. I once assumed it meant estrogen was too high. It doesn't always.

In my case, estrogen levels often appeared "normal" on paper. What made estrogen dominant was context. Progesterone was insufficient to counterbalance it. Estrogen receptors remained active without regulation. Tissue was being stimulated without protection.

When I was diagnosed as estrogen dominant, it was alongside ovarian cysts. That was not incidental. Ovarian cysts often form when ovulation occurs without strong luteal support. The follicle does not resolve properly. Progesterone production is weak or absent, and estrogen remains locally active.

For years, I was told that because my cycles were regular, PCOS wasn't likely. That assumption is outdated. There is a phenotype, sometimes called ovulatory or estrogen-dominant PCOS, where cycles are predictable, ovulation occurs, but progesterone remains chronically inadequate.

My history of miscarriage requiring progesterone support confirmed that this pattern existed long before perimenopause ever arrived.

Progesterone Was Always the Missing Piece

Every miscarriage I experienced carried the same message:
progesterone was too low to sustain pregnancy.

Years later, lab testing showed progesterone and testosterone at ground-level low; low enough to be alarming.

This wasn't new.

It was simply visible.

Progesterone is often framed as a fertility hormone, something necessary only if pregnancy is the goal. That framing misses its true role.

Progesterone is protective.

It protects breast tissue from unchecked estrogen signaling.

It protects the endometrium from hyperplasia.

It steadies the nervous system.

It supports sleep, bone remodeling, and immune balance.

Choosing not to pursue pregnancy did not erase my body's need for progesterone. It only removed fertility from the conversation, and unfortunately, many clinicians stop listening there.

What the Numbers Were Quietly Saying

My A1C of 5.6 was technically normal. It was also deeply informative.

That number sits at the upper edge of optimal and is common in estrogen-dominant PCOS. It reflects mild insulin resistance or stress-mediated glucose dysregulation, not enough to disrupt ovulation, but enough to impair luteal hormone production.

Insulin resistance suppresses the corpus luteum. When the corpus luteum underperforms, progesterone suffers.

That explains why I ovulated, why my cycles were predictable, and why progesterone never rose adequately, allowing estrogen to remain dominant.

This metabolic–hormonal interaction likely shaped my body for decades before perimenopause ever arrived.

Perimenopause Did Not Create the Problem

Perimenopause did not introduce chaos out of nowhere.

It removed compensation.

As ovarian reserve declined, estrogen peaks became erratic. Progesterone output—already low, collapsed. Testosterone fell to near zero.

In some women, this creates dramatic symptoms. In others, it creates numbness.

My body stopped giving warnings because the hormonal contrast disappeared. Estrogen no longer surged cleanly. Progesterone no longer attempted to rise. The cycle flattened.

The absence of symptoms was not healing.

It was endocrine quiet.

When Sensation Returned

Wild yam cream does not contain progesterone. The body cannot convert it into progesterone.

And yet, after a month of use, something changed.

Breast tenderness returned.

Nipple sensitivity resurfaced.

My body began speaking again.

That did not mean balance was restored. It meant estrogen signaling had become more perceptible.

Wild yam can influence estrogen receptor sensitivity and adrenal pathways. In a body with estrogen dominance and no progesterone buffer, that can amplify estrogen effects.

What I felt was not protection.

It was contrast without cover.

I knew instinctively to pause.

Why I Paused

Pausing the wild yam cream was not failure.

It was discernment.

Without progesterone onboard, anything that increases estrogen signaling, even subtly returns the body to a familiar but risky pattern: sensation without safety.

Stepping back allowed my baseline to re-establish. It let me observe whether tenderness faded, whether sensitivity subsided, whether my body returned to its quieter rhythm. That information mattered.

In endocrine health, restraint is often more powerful than intervention.

A Necessary Clarification

What I am describing here is my body, not every woman's.

Low progesterone was central to my story, but it was not the only factor. I also lived with low thyroid function and Lyme disease, both of which place chronic stress on the endocrine system. Together, they likely shaped my fertility in ways that will not apply to another woman reading these pages.

Another woman's infertility may stem from insulin resistance.

Another's from a pituitary tumor.

Another may have carried a child once and never conceived again.

Another may have no clear explanation at all.

The causes are not interchangeable.

The common thread is not diagnosis; it is silence.

I did not know what questions I was allowed to ask. I trusted that patterns would be seen for me, that someone would explain why repeated loss mattered, why progesterone support was necessary, why my body kept trying but could not sustain.

This is why I tell my own story.

Not to diagnose anyone else.

Not to offer a formula.

But to show what can be missed when symptoms are treated in isolation and context is ignored.

What I Know Now

Unopposed estrogen is not dangerous because estrogen exists. It becomes dangerous when progesterone is absent.

Progesterone is not about youth.

It is not cosmetic.

It is protective.

My body was not betraying me with tenderness. It was communicating exposure.

Fear is not preventive. Suppression without understanding creates new problems. What reduces risk is buffering, metabolic clarity, inflammation control, proper elimination, and adequate progesterone signaling.

I am not late.

I am aware.

And awareness, paired with understanding, is one of the most powerful forms of care a woman can have.

Notes

ACKNOWLEDGMENTS

1   Note to the Reader: Throughout this book, you may have noticed that I use "G-D" and Hashem in place of G-D. This is because the use of G-D's name is considered sacred in Jewish tradition, and out of respect, many Jews prefer to use alternative names or titles when referring to the divine. Additionally, in the time period of the story, Hannah and Elkanah would have used various names and titles to refer to G-D, including Adonai, Elohim, Jireh, and Hashem, depending on the context and the aspect of G-D's character they were addressing. I have chosen to use "G-D" or L-rd to honor both Jewish tradition and the historical context of the story. You can learn more about the names of G-D from Kay Arthur's book: "Lord I Want to Know You" as well as this website that lists the many different names used for God: How to See Many Amazing Names of God - NewCREEations

There is also some great content that I did research on to flesh out my characters of Hannah and Peninnah. You can read it here: Barren Women in the Bible | Jewish Women's Archive (jwa.org)

You can also see where I drew out some of my commentary between Elkhana and Yosef from this website; and how in the bible study I addressed the idea of Adoption as a way to expand on ones family: What Does the Bible Say About Infertility? - Biblical Archaeology Society

2   While this book is based on the story of Hannah found in the Bible, I have taken some creative liberties to bring the story to life. I have drawn on various sources, including the Midrash and Aggadah, and used my imagination to flesh out the characters and scenes. However, I have done my best to stay true to the essence of the story and to honor its message. While I used Bible verses throughout the story, they are not necessarily in canonical order. You will find anachronisms throughout the story, as this is not meant to be historically. It is my telling in a historical fiction. I used certain verses, including ones from the book of Revelation as well as Psalms, to enhance the story and make it more impactful, even though they may not have been known or read by the people in Hannah's time, and they are not in historical order.

It is important to me that my readers acknowledge the sources from which I have drawn, and that I clarify any changes or adaptations that I have made to the original material. I want to be sure that I have honored the essence of the story while making it engaging for modern readers. I have also tried to do my best to give credit and acknowledgment to the various authors or content creators with whom I found my historical data and cultural information.

If anything was missed by accident I will make a new addition with the corrections. I didn't intentionally misrepresent anyone.

Verse used throughout the story:

Chapter 1 Verses: ^1 I John 4:18; ^2 Song of Solomon 4:1-4; ^4 Jeremiah 33:10; ^5 Revelation 19:7; ^7 Proverbs 3:6

Chapter 2

Verses: ^8 Song of Solomon 1:17

Chapter 3 Verses: ^11 Psalm 57:7-10; ^12 Jeremiah 17:14; ^13 Psalm 51:10 ^14 Psalm 73:26;

Chapter 4 Verses: ^16 Isaiah 55:8-9; ^17 Psalm 8:3-4; ^18 Psalm 8:5-9; ^19 Psalm 31:9; ^20 Lamentations 3:31-33; ^21 Lamentations 3:20-23; ^22 Psalm 27:13-14

Chapter 5 Verses: ^24 Psalm 143:8,10

Chapter 6 Verses: ^25 Proverbs 3:5-6; ^26 Jeremiah 29:11 ^27 Psalm 127:4-5; ^28 Deuteronomy 8:2; ^29 Genesis 1:28; ^30 Genesis 25:21;

Chapter 7 Verses: ^31 Hebrews 11:1-12; ^32 1 Corinthians 2:9; ^33 Matthew 19:4-6;

Chapter 9 Verses: ^35 Isaiah 41:10

Chapter 11 Verses ^36 Psalm 91:2 ^37 Isaiah 40:31 ^38 1 Samuel 2:6-7

Chapter 12 Verses ^41 1 Samuel 1:11; ^42 1 Samuel 1:12-18; ^43 1 Samuel 1:23; ^44 1 Samuel 1:26-28; ^45 1 Samuel 2:20;

AFTERWORD

3   **The Plan of Salvation:**

The story of Hannah is rich with the story of redemption and grace. In it we see how G-D intervenes in her life to fulfill his ultimate plan for Israel. Samuel was a great prophet who led his people back to G-D. We see how Hannah gave up her right to him, for the betterment of Israel. She did not fully understand G-D's plan. But she trusted Him.

We see where HaShem (G-D) also gives his only son Yeshua (Jesus) for all of humanity. He sent Mary, a young virgin, a message that would change her life. Through the Angel Gabriel, she was told that she would have a son who would be the savior of the whole world. Yeshua would lead people back to G-D.

HaShem wants a relationship with you! In the beginning He always had a plan to redeem humanity. But it is up to us to take his perfect gift. We do not have to accept it. We can leave it and peruse our own wants and desires. The consequence of this choice is hell, which was never created for human beings. Hell was created for the devil and his fallen angels. But G-D is holy, and He cannot allow sin into His paradise. And so, the only way to live eternally in peace is by accepting Yeshua, His son, as your savior. You absolutely can choose not to do this. We have free will which is a gift from G-D. But the choice to not take the gift has a consequence tied to it. That is Hell. There are always two choices. One for the good, and one for evil. Or better put, you can choose of a blessing or a curse. The blessing is taking the Son, Yeshua as your savior. The curse is choosing not to take Him. But it ultimately land on you.

In this life we will have troubles and trials of many degrees. But if you have Yeshua as your savior, you have a hope. You have a promise that He has control, though you do not understand it. You will have a peace that surpasses all understanding. But there will always be struggle on this side of Heaven to remain in that peace. It is a daily giving up of your own self, by putting your hope in Yehsua to guide you through the day. Tomorrow will have its own troubles. He is sufficient for today. Take heart, He has overcome the world, and death. Though we die, we can live, if we make him our L-rd and Savior. The prayer below is not a magic prayer or potion. But it is an example. If you believe in your heart and confess with your mouth that Yeshua (Jesus) is L-rd and ask him to save you, He will!

Prayer: "Dear L-rd, I know that I need a savior. I am desperate for your grace and that you will fill me with your Spirit. I believe that you died on the cross for my sins, and you rose again on the third day to victory. Please come into my life, be my boss, L-rd and savior. In your name Jesus, (Yeshua) I pray, Amen"

John 1:11-13; John 3:16; John 10:27-28; Romans 8:28-30; Ephesians 2:8-10;
    Isaiah 53:5-6; Titus 2:11-14; 1 Peter 1:3-5

About the Author

Melissa Allred is a passionate author, animal lover, and stay-at-home mom with a talent for weaving compelling stories. With a heart for encouraging women in their faith. Melissa has written seven books that draw readers into the beauty and struggle of life. Her second work, Hannah, explores the powerful story of a woman who yearned for a child and the incredible faith that sustained her through her darkest moments. As a homeschooling mother, Melissa understands the demands of busy family life and believes that everyone has a story worth telling. Through her writing, Melissa seeks to inspire her readers to live with hope, purpose, and faith.

Thank you for taking the time to learn more about me and my work. If you enjoyed reading 'Hannah' and want to stay up-to-date on my future projects, I invite you to follow me on Instagram @mallredbooks. You can also visit my website https://substack.com/@mallred5 for more information about my writing journey and to sign up for my newsletter.

I look forward to connecting with you!

You can connect with me on:

🌐 https://www.tiktok.com/@mallred5

🔗 https://www.instagram.com/mallredbooks?igsh=MTYwZHVpemmk1aWpiaQ==&utm_source=ig_contact_invite

Subscribe to my newsletter:

✉ https://substack.com/@mallred5

Also by Melissa Allred

Widows Ranch

A contemporary story of loss, resilience, and unexpected community, centered on women brought together through shared hardship and the slow work of healing.

Phoenix Queen

An epic tale of rebirth and strength, blending fantasy and symbolism as a wounded heroine rises from devastation into purpose, identity, and power.

Daughter of Eve

A reflective, faith-driven work examining womanhood, legacy, and redemption through a biblical lens, inviting readers to reconsider identity, calling, and grace.

Utterly Unprepared

A practical, honest guide for homesteaders and animal keepers, offering real-life lessons learned through experience, faith, and perseverance, especially for those raising goats and livestock.

Elisabeth

A reverent biblical fiction inspired by the life of Elisabeth, capturing the beauty of obedience, waiting, and God's faithfulness in seasons of silence and fulfillment.

The Princess and Her Owl

https://www.goodreads.com/book/show/131105503-
the-princess-and-her-owl?from_search=true&from_
srp=true&qid=IZBHf1Cqg5&rank=3

Princess Amrie is loved by all in the kingdom of Barinash. Her beauty, intelligence, and skill with a bow make her the envy of many. But trouble is brewing in the kingdom, and Amrie must step up to protect her people. With the help of her friends, she uncovers a plot that threatens to destroy everything she holds dear. Will she be able to save her kingdom and the people she loves? Find out in this thrilling tale of adventure, friendship, and heroism.

www.ingramcontent.com/pod-product-compliance
Lightning Source LLC
Chambersburg PA
CBHW031430130726
47989CB00003B/1081